PROVIDENCE

A Story of Hope

Also by

June E. Summers

Grandma's Orchard: A Harvest of Poetry

PROVIDENCE

A Story of Hope

June E. Summers

Park Point Press | Golden, Colorado

Park Point Press
573 Park Point Drive
Golden, Colorado 80401-7402

Cover design, book layout & typesetting
Maria Robinson, Designs On You, LLC.
Littleton, Colorado 80121
Set in 11 point Chaparral Pro

Printed in the United States of America
Published June 2016

ISBN 978-0-917849-47-3

Like you, the world already has what it needs to be perfect.
Some have feared the healing of our world because
they have equated healing with ending. But this could not be so.
All healing is a beginning.
The resurrection of our life will come not through
destruction, but through transformation.
The caterpillar does not die; it becomes something entirely new
and more wonderful. To hold our world in the willingness
to have it continue to live, and to acknowledge that
such a world already lives within our hearts,
is the greatest gift that you and I can offer to our planet.

~ Alan Cohen
"The Healing of The Planet Earth"

"For I am about to create new heavens and a new Earth;
the former things shall not be remembered or come to mind.
But be glad and rejoice forever in what I am creating."

~ Isaiah 65:17-18

Contents

Preface vix

Acknowledgments x

One Round-Trip, Please 1

Doors of Time 9

The Shadowlands 17

School Daze 27

A Mark of Time 35

New Beginnings 45

Strange Winds A-Blowin' 53

The Dark Prince 61

Together We Stand 69

The Messenger 77

Farewells and Hellos 89

Fearful Illusions 99

Caught In The Balance 109

The Dream 117

The Day Time Blinked 125

Exit The Dark 133

Welcome To Providence 145

The Reunion 157

Afterword 169

About The Author 171

Preface

IF IT IS TRUTH that nothing is by chance, this book in your hand is there for a reason.

If it is truth that we have the gift of "free will," you can choose to read this book to the last page or stop at any time. If you stop before the end, please dismiss anything you have read up to that point. But, if you do read to the last page, this author feels it should allow you, the reader, to greet all the awaiting tomorrows with courage and hopefulness.

The truth of this story is not whether it is even true or not. Reality is your perception of it. If you see the future as threatening, you are holding on to illusions for: "Nothing real can be threatened, nothing unreal exists. Herein lies the peace of God." *(A Course In Miracles)*

~ June E. Summers

Acknowledgments

AS A CHILD GROWING UP in an organized religious environment, I had to conform my thought process to what I was taught. I have since realized that my own spiritual being is who I am, and I presently don't fear my God. I believe "God is love!" I also believe we are all created by the same Creator no matter of race, religion, intellect, monetary, or political positions.

This book came to light after being misplaced for several years. My grandson, Dan, put some of the beginning editing touches to it and my daughter, Kristi, and I completed the task. This book has been like a work in progress until now. I wrote it at a time when fear of impending world disasters was newly being considered as a reality. I did not want to play into fear, as I believe the changes in our world have always been and will perhaps always be. Rebirth is eminent, but fear need not!

I thank my family for reminding me daily that love conquers fear. And, long after this author of 84 years has graduated this earthly plane, I will still have gratification, feeling that I have left behind a story that is full of hope for their tomorrows.

~ June E. Summers

PROVIDENCE

A Story of Hope

1

One Round-Trip, Please

INSTEAD OF FALL, people now referred to the present season as the "Wind Season," and the prevailing northwesterly winds had created an almost cloudless night. The heavens appeared to be diamond studded and their brilliance magnified by the velvet blackness of the sky. It evoked a sense of timelessness to the passenger inhabiting seat 215 of Air Transport United. The cushy, reclining seats and the transparent dome of the aircraft provided the means of enhancing this panoramic view of the night-magic to any interested participants.

The craft was beginning its descent and the view outside was now being divided with another spectacular scene. The passenger in seat 215's attention was being compelled earthward as another light show was entering the awareness stage. This dazzling display of light colors and intensities all but dimmed the brightness of the stars. It was breathtaking!

Air vehicles of different sizes were streaking or hovering over the city in what appeared to be a very ordered and controlled manipulation. There was a variety of intersecting laser beams lighting illusionary roadways for the vehicles to pursue. It all resembled an aerial ballet being performed to entertain the airborne passengers of the craft. Yet, even their compelling performances were lost to the magnificence of the Earth display taking place in center ring! Ground vehicles resembled iridescent strings of pearls being teased across a black, velvet gown. Then, as the craft lowered itself closer to Mother Earth, she seemed to celebrate its coming with a spectacular, awe-inspiring masterpiece of futuristic beauty! The unique shapes and sizes of the white granite and glass buildings illuminated and reflecting the night lights of the city made a utopian setting that seemed almost mystical.

The Captain's voice interrupted the spellbound passenger in seat 215. He alerted them to the soon linking with Providence's Air Terminal platform, hoped their flight had been pleasant, and advised the outer climate surrounding the city was a brisk 62 degrees; which was expected during Wind Season.

Passenger 215 returned her attention to the now approaching lights of the city of Providence, but her attention was directed more inward than to the outer visualizations. She knew this was a first time arrival at this particular place. She also was aware of this being her first air travel in over some twenty to thirty years. Her aging, physical body reasoned all this, but somewhere inside her mental awareness another reasoning was taking place. Her inner-child was frolicking around and shouting, "See, I knew this was a real place and I wasn't just a wishing!" It was like a homesick child that suddenly found herself in the arms of her loving parent. Dana glanced around quickly to see if any of the other passengers had caught a glimpse of this silly, old woman acting like a free-spirit child. How could she even explain to her adult, so-in-control mind—this sudden burst of happy abandonment? Yet, the child-within was totally convincing her present illogical mind she had mentally experienced this exact moment in a previous time and space existence. She had felt the same emotional wonderment then as now.

Then, Dana remembered the special trip to Epcot with her son, Devon. Was it really twenty-five years ago? How much had transpired since then and yet seemed only yesterday.

Dana had awakened early, showered and dressed, and was anxiously waiting for her son and his wife to pick her up to start out for Epcot. She had looked forward to this trip for years, but always postponed because of finances or other pressing responsibilities. Not any longer, this time she was going and not even the below normal cold would dampen the excitement of the day's expected adventure.

As they walked into the first attraction, the magic began. Dana was a somewhat conservative, reserved type person at least outwardly. Inwardly, there was always that creative child tat believed in dreams coming true, and perhaps an adventurer that dared to follow those dreams or even to be a builder of dreams. Dana also felt that perhaps time is but a concept to enable man to categorize his learning stages into an understandable order. Perhaps there really is no units or separation, but that past and future are but expansions of the now. Maybe that's why Dana felt she had existed on earth's plane before, and in some form perhaps existing in future space that now is creating. Epcot seemed to be opening doors of awareness not visited in her mind before, or at least, not for ages.

Dana was engrossed with a simulated ride portraying Earth's development. Watching the origin of Earth unfold was a spiritual experience, one that she felt in some other than physical form she had been privileged to witness. It was almost the feeling of giving birth and watching a home video of your child's first interactions with its world. You feel smugness because you were there to observe even though you were just an on-looker. The pre-historic simulation aroused much the same emotions that included awe and wonderment. May times through the various culturally-based or historically inclined simulations and movies, very strong bonds brought about with a sense of familiarity to the settings or the people made Dana wonder if she had physically interacted in any of these time and being spaces. The whole day took on "a many lifetime" education. The smorgasbord of mental feasting that was laid out to Dana that day was like a gourmet, open house, mind storehouse...there for the savoring.

Dana had totally allowed her Inner-child free reign of the day. She was functioning on "Possibilities" and not logic. So when they sat in this moving cart and were taken through this passageway depicting the evolution of transportation, Dana was no longer a logical-being. She became associated with each and every simulation being presented. Then came the magic-carpet ride! The carrier they were being conveyed through this attraction appeared to be in some sort of aircraft soaring through this star studded blackness. It appeared to be nosing downward and then, far below but quickly approaching, was the most breath-taking sight of Dana's memory. A futuristic gem-stone and crystal city, real and existing—and we were approaching it as if for a landing. "Yes, Yes, Yes, I knew you were not just a figment of my imagination! You are a possibility and I will land for real one day at your air terminal! I will, I will!" the little child Dana shouted with glee.

The whole day at Epcot created magical memories Dana would pack away in her memory chest. She would relive that splendid adventure many times. She knew she would add many more happy memories to her chest, and perhaps a few not-so-happy, but still special. She might even in time forget a lot of these special moments...at least until something happens to trigger an old memory and bring it back to life. But, isn't that the magic of it all?

2

Doors of Time

DANA STOOD AT THE OPEN DOOR of her Florida home watching her son Devon loading the last of his personal belongings into the rented truck. Once again, the doors of life were performing their opening and closing duty. How many times Dana had opened up to new surprises or watched a closing with sadness. Just as quickly as a door slamming shut or swinging open, Dana's life had encompassed change. That strong, gentle, good-looking man stepping into the U-Haul with that familiar, warm grin spreading across his face as he waved to his mom had his share of revolving doors also.

He remembered another moving van and the waving goodbye to people that had been a part of his first seven years. He had hated leaving his special friend, and then; there were his alternate parents, Grandpa and Grandma Barton. Mom had decided those Missouri winters were no longer appealing, and after a vacation to Florida...well, "Florida, here come the Bartons!" He also remembered feeling very anxious as he stepped inside this house he was now leaving. Anxious thoughts like, "Will I ever find a friend like Jody? Will I ever see Gramps and Grandmother again? And will they forget me?" This time as he pulled away from the home of some twenty years, he again felt a little anxious. It was taking a backseat to the excitement he was also feeling over moving finally into his very own home. He chuckled and patted the blue-jeaned knee of the petite, young beauty by his side. Tamara squeezed her husband's hand as they shared a very happy moment. They'd go back later and pick up baby, Derek.

Dana also remembered feeling very anxious the first time she'd opened this door she was now standing in. "Will I be able to make a justifiable living here? Will Devon accept this new living arrangement? Will I make new friends easily?" As these thoughts attacked her consciousness, they heralded a river of anxieties. She recalled feeling very alone and vulnerable. She felt somewhat the same feeling now as then. She had shared living quarters with her son for thirty-some years, and for the most part; their roommate arrangement had been very compatible. Now she was facing being a "single-act" again, and for the first time in ever so long; Dana thought about her husband, and missed him deeply.

Dana's memory took a trip back to the doorway of her Missouri home. She had just realized she was a "single-act" then, too. In her mind, she visualized this ever-so-handsome man in an Army uniform. He had a way of displaying this boyish grin that always won any argument Dana and her husband had. He had used that tactic when he explained why he felt it his duty to go with some of the enlisted NCOs of his company to serve as advisors in Vietnam. They had just purchased and moved into their new home, and Dana had just been informed by her doctor that she was pregnant. This was a dream during into a nightmare. All of Dana's pleading and coy persuasion efforts were invalidated by Dean's desire to serve his country... and that boyish grin! Dean had assured her, he would be back before the baby came. He kept that promise, but it brought sorrow instead of joy. One month before Devon was born, Dana received the honor of his flag that had draped his casket. He sleeps in a Missouri National Cemetery. Dana felt so alone and abandoned.

Devon had become the hub of Dana's life, her very reason for existing. Now he was moving on to a life of his own, and Dana wondered if she would find a new reason for living?

Devon drove the U-Haul down the familiar streets he'd grown up on and past the school he had graduated from some years ago. He recalled the good and not-so-good times spent in that building. He was not a bad student, but just so full of exuberance that it had caused the principal and him to share a few confrontational moments. He'd excelled in woodwork class and even went on to do a couple years at local Vo-Tech. He was now making a good living at numerous remodeling or repair jobs, and also worked for a construction firm.

It was at the construction site that he had met Tamara, his wife. She was the bookkeeper for the firm. She was friendly, but quite reserved...almost shy. She was a petite, dark-haired beauty that reminded Devon of a China doll. After only two dates, Devon knew he'd be asking her to be his wife. Eight months later they shared vows at a beautiful, sunset, lakeside wedding-ceremony.

They had moved in with Dana so as to be able to save enough to buy their own home. A year later, Tamara took a short work leave to give birth to their son, Derek.

Dana really felt alive again babysitting her grandson so his mommy could go back to work. He was such an alert, good-natured baby. Dana knew this child would play an important part in her life and in his world.

Dana also knew her happiness was about to be altered a little though when Devon and Tamara being home searching on their weekends. She tried to join in their excitement as they voiced their pleasure in finding this older, two-story farmhouse with twenty acres of grazing and woodlands. It had citrus and nut trees, a garden area, a little barn, and a pond stocked with fish. It was a dream, but to Dana it felt like a nightmare about to ascend on her present happy state-of-being. This fear was squelching the non-verbal message she wanted to send to her son.

Devon tried over and over to convince his mother to rent or sell this place and come live with them—there was plenty of room. Dana was almost tempted, but couldn't quite cut the memory cord that was attached to all the living that had transpired here. Devon assured her, they were just a call away; and that he'd make daily checks on her. Those emptied rooms would be a problem emotionally and so Dana began an almost obsessive redecorating endeavor. At least the kids were leaving Derek's old crib for visiting times. Dana watched the moving truck disappear out of sight, slowly closed the door, and directed her numb body to Derek's crib to check on him. She would miss him the most, she thought. He lay there sleeping soundly, oblivious to all the changes about to happen in his life. His doors were just beginning to swing...but for now it mattered little to him.

Tamara had quit work to help with the remodeling of the farm, and even though it was almost completed; she declined going back to work. It was so exciting doing all the things she had never had time for before. She was also enjoying being a full-time mother and watching Derek take first steps and learning to talk. They had done wonders to the farm, and even Dana was spending more time out there. Tamara was pregnant again and Derek was just at the "terrible," busy-two's stage and wore mommy out fast. Besides Grandma's were a lot more fun these days. Tamara appreciated Dana's help and they began to form a friendship they never allowed to develop before.

Dana was even beginning to enjoy the quietness of her evenings alone in her own home. She was able to read and attend to her "inner" needs. She felt that this was a special time for her that allowed herself personal time without feeling guilty over neglecting other-responsibilities. As she tuned out those busy outside noises and thoughts and slid quietly into her inner-chambers, she discovered reservoirs of hidden strengths, courage, and dreams she never knew existed. She reasoned there was a purpose to this existence, and if she just dared to live this life to its fullest...it would manifest untold wonderment. She knew that even through the scary changes, this "innerness" would walk her through it unscathed. She also realized that each important person in her life had a given plan for their life that was unfolding. They cold never complete or halt another's destiny. They could enjoy the time their travels intertwined...and that was what she planned to do.

It was a brisk, fall morning when Dana was awaked by the sound of a phone ringing. Devon sounded excited and a little panicky. He informed Dana that he was bringing Derek over, and then they hoped to beat the stork to the hospital. They did, and about six hours later; Devon called again. He proudly announced the arrival of his daughter, Joy Dean. Dean was in honor of the father he never got to know, but loved.

These were really the best of all times for both households. Dana enjoyed her grandmother's role as much as her selfish, quiet times. She really was adding special events to her memory chest. She often though of how many times she'd opened that front door to welcome friends or to say goodbye to a loved one. Time has a way of balancing all things though, and presently the scale was tipped to the positive side. Dana knew in all probability the scales would tip back and forth a few more times in her life. She was not as afraid of change as she once was. That was the excitement of living, wondering what was waiting behind the door. Anyway, yesterdays doors were already shut; tomorrow's remained unopened, but today she'd walk out that front door and welcome "her" now with open arms. She knew it awaited her with goodness, her "innerness" had promised it so.

3

The Shadowlands

DEVON WALKED OVER and switched off the television set. "What a bunch of 'malarkey' they were spouting," he mumbled. The TV newscaster was making reference to the President's state-of-the-Union address of the night before. Devon had listened to that also and felt just as disillusioned with the state-of affairs then as now. "How can they declare the healthy and solid status of the economy when people were barely able to eke out a living? How ridiculous to be urging people to invest in America's future when tier own future looked so bleak?"

Devon poured another cup of coffee, wandered out on to his front porch, and slid into a vacant rocker. He still felt very grateful for this beautiful home site he'd purchased for him and his family. Yet, there was this feeling of uneasiness that it could all disappear and he would be powerless to prevent it from happening. Tamara and he had invested a lot of time, effort, and money the last five years. Now, just when it was in top-market working order, their monetary flow was preventing them from enjoying its potential.

Interest rates had climbed again and at 18 to 22% for home loans, no one was buying, selling, or building homes. This was closing down a lot of contractors including the firm Devon worked for. The odd remodeling or repair jobs were few and far between as most were doing things themselves or letting them go because of money scarcity.

Even though interest rates were also high on "plastic" money, in these hard times they were safer to carry than cash. The "have-nots" and drug users had all but made carrying cash so unsafe it was an obsolete monetary system. So everyone was over-extending themselves with credit cards. That's what happened when Tamara tried to buy a much-needed pair of shoes for Joy Dean. The clerk apologized but reported the computer would not accept her card as it had exceeded the allowable credit.

Their gas cards were all but maxed out. Gas was such a luxury at $3.20 a gallon and higher for hi-test. So other than driving for necessities, you walked or stayed home.

Devon couldn't find work so he took care of the farm and the children. Tamara had located this waitress job just a few miles from home so it wouldn't be so expensive to drive to and from. It was an evening job and Devon felt some alarm over that, what with the rampart crime conditions. They all had to do whatever they had to, though these were times to test man's (and woman's) soul.

Derek would be starting school this fall and that was another worry. Because of transportation costs, buses only ran twice a week, Monday morning and Friday afternoon. The children stayed in school dorms during the week. Derek was excited, but his parents felt he was so young to be away from them for such long periods. A lot of parents were doing home tutoring. With Tamara working, this just didn't seem a viable option.

Dana was feeling anxious, too. She had been living very comfortably on her window's pension and the savings she'd accrued from her years as a dental technician. She'd paid cash for her home from Dean's insurance settlements. Now though, her pension had been severely cut back, plus cost-of-living index was on the rise so she was constantly having to dip into her dwindling savings to just meet monthly living expenses. She'd all but "maxed out" her credit cards helping out the kids. Still she knew that his too would pass and things would be good for them again someday. That "inner" reservoir was sure being visited a lot these days though. She was most grateful to know it was there waiting for her and inexhaustible. A lot of people were really getting discouraged and even giving up and checking out of life entirely. She didn't see Devon and the grandchildren very often as everyone found visiting by phone cheaper than driving. She missed them and sometimes would give into that "lonesome" state of feeling again, but never for long. There was too much living to do.

Dana did find a way to bring in a little extra cash. She started a day care in her home for working moms in her housing area. She charged the minimum amount so as to help her neighbors. They in return would bring in eatables to help with her grocery bills.

Terrorism was making the news again, too. Little countries were threatening the bigger ones—the old have more" and "have less" competition. There was a news bulletin Devon and Tamara were just discussing about this self-proclaimed, little-god dictator from a newly formed African province. It seemed he was threatening nuclear retaliation if his province was not recognized. It had shown him on the screen, a large, burly-looking man draped in satin and gold robes with a blue-satin turban wrapped around his head and fastened with a diamond brooch. Tamara felt alarmed because she was brought up in a very strict, Pentecostal-type church; and remembered hearing a description of an anti-Christ figure closely resembling this man. Devon tried to assure her there was no connection, but "who knows," he wondered. Devon recalled this conversation and what with the newscast of the morning, he just shook his head and assured himself that this world was sure in a heap of trouble. He was still muttering as he walked back into the kitchen for a coffee refill.

Unbeknownst to the majority of the world citizens, governments too were concerned with the sick condition of their planet and were presently meeting in a secret place to discuss solutions. It seemed the monetary exchange was the most pressing issue. Any feasible plan to correct this corrupt, non-usable monetary system would have to be implemented on a worldwide basis for maximum control. That way, selected guardians or administrators cold separate the deserving participants from the undesirables. All recognized countries would be participants and the others would either be coerced into staying in line or become isolated. Deserving citizens would have access, but others would be banned, therefore eliminating the crime factor. The idea of individual credit reserves for business establishments, corporations, and even individuals to be housed in global banking units across the world interconnected seemed plausible.

This would be a totally computerized system that would respond only to an individualized, implanted identification chip. It was decided to implant the microchip into the back of the right hand and one into the forehead as a backup. They would start with twenty-one year old adults at first, then the eighteen and up. The adults would be allowed extra credits for each dependent not yet of age or physically dependent. As each citizen reaches eighteen or wishes to participate in any acceptable employment, an implant would be required. Included in the individual's microchip records would be an updated personal file for public viewing. This was to weed undesirables out of the public mainstream. There would be a grace period of one year for each designated district to accomplish this. Each citizen would be given three deadline opportunities to comply before "rejection" notice.

The ordinary drones of the World Beehive were totally unaware of what had just transpired. They were busy trying to juggle their present monetary units in order to rob Peter to pay Paul.

Devon rinsed his coffee cup, checked on the kids playing on the big tire swing he'd built for them in the backyard, decided to jaunt on out to the mailbox. He avoided this walk most days because he always came back with a handful of overdue bills. He tried to get out of the "funk" mood that had settled in on him all morning. He watched the sunlight playing hide-and-seek through the branches of the trees only to skip and play on the ground around his feet. He watched the birds flitter from branch to branch sending happy messages to the world. He even stopped to pick a few wild flowers to put on the table to surprise Tamara when she awoke. He felt ashamed for being so "down" when there was so much beauty and love surrounding him just waiting to be absorbed...and it was free!

He opened the door of the mailbox and was even whistling an old favorite tune as he pulled out a couple envelopes. He'd read them later; this feeling was too good to dampen with unwelcome news.

He put the letters on the table, selected a pretty vase for the flowers, set them on the table, and joined the kids outside. He enlisted their help, which they eagerly agreed to, in working in "Mom's Garden." He'd promised to care for it while Tamara was working. It was her pride and joy. She'd even taken a few ribbons for her produce at the County Fair. She always said it would reward them for their efforts someday. It was already doing that with supplying most of their eatables. Along with eggs from their chickens, a little meat from the farm animals, and the garden, the Bartons at least never went to bed hungry. Tamara was even learning how to bake bread, and so food wise they were fairly independent.

Tamara got up a little before noon. She just couldn't sleep well in the daytime even though her body was still tired from her evening waitress shift. Besides, she missed interacting with her family. She didn't like the people who frequented the restaurant where she worked. It wasn't "ritzy" enough for high-class patronage, and the working class couldn't afford the luxury of dining out that much. Mostly her clients were those who had not "earned" their pay, but had acquired it illegally or stolen it. They were an overbearing, cocky crowd and Tamara was always uncomfortable around them. It did help with home finances and even though the hourly pay was minimum, the restaurant patrons were fairly good "tippers." She reasoned it made them feel superior.

Tamara grabbed a cup and finished the dredges of coffee Devon had left in the pot. She walked over and sat down at the table. She touched and smelled the wild flowers, a smile drifted across her face. She picked up the mail laid on the table and noticed one was form the bank. She dreaded opening it, and just holding it made the pit of her stomach feel queasy. "Here goes nothing," she announced as she ripped open the envelope. There it was, the bomb! "This is to inform you that you are now four months past due on our mortgage loan. We are sorry, but unless a payment is received by next payment due date, foreclosure is inevitable." "Devon," Tamara raised her weak voice to its highest pitch. "Can you please come here a moment?" Tamara was always so in control, but she felt like she was caught up in a whirlpool that was sucking her into a blackness. She felt herself falling down, down... Devon rushed in to find his wife slumped in a faint on the table still holding this letter in her limp hand.

Dana, Devon and Tamara sat at the long table in the bank waiting for the paperwork to be completed. Devon was still urging his mom to reconsider. He felt he'd really let his whole family down. Dana reassured him she'd been planning to do this for quite some time as she missed them all so much, and preferred to be out at the farm with them.

Mr. Ross, the vice president of the bank, sat down with the completed papers and reviewed their contents before asking for signatures. Dana said she understood that her signature would give ownership of her home to the bank, and that the cash settlement (which was ridiculously low) would go to pay past due loan debts on the farm mortgage plus a five-year, paid-in-advance arrangement. Like Dana told Devon, "In five years we'll be on top again, I just know. Besides, it will be good to have roommates again!"

Dana watched as the rented U-Haul pulled away and headed for the farm with a few of her cherished belongings. The other things she had sold cheaply, given, or traded to neighbors. She once more walked through vacant rooms and said goodbye to memory ghosts. She didn't linger that long this time, as she was anxious to begin her new living adventure. She locked the front door, drove to the bank, and delivered the key to Mr. Ross. Then, she headed for the farm. Even though this was not the best of times, Dana knew this too was but a small piece of the big picture that was her life. She accepted it as such knowing that it was only a few brushstrokes on the masterpiece she was creating. Since she knew the completed masterpiece would be good, and this was a part of it...only goodness could come from this. She sighed and looked out at the sky. The sun was just peeping out from behind a cloud, it smiled at Dana, and Dana smiled back.

4

School Daze

DEREK WAS WIDE-AWAKE and impatiently trying to get his grandmother to get up and join him in his enthusiasm to ready himself for his first day of school. Dana tried very hard to display a measure of Derek's elation, but was difficult as she was really dreading his departing the home for such long periods.

It sure was different than Dana's or even Devon's school days. Now the government didn't enforce school attendance. It just didn't have the necessary funds to provide adequate educational services anymore. Public schools weren't the most desirable choices of learning institutions. Besides, having your child "farmed out" for a week at a time was causing parents concern. Those financially able were either driving their children to private schools or installing home computer educational systems. Quite a few of the "old" middle class chose to become home tutors. This required the parent to be learned enough in certain required areas, could purchase a tutor certificate for fifty dollars. This had to be renewed annually. Dana decided she would try for this in case Derek's school adventure was not successful. Besides, their little girl would soon be school age, and the idea of her being away from them at night was not an adventure the family wished to embark on.

"Beep, Beep." "Come On, Derek, let's go get on your bus." Devon called to his first-born. He wrapped his big, protective hand around that little one nestled so trustingly in his, and carried Derek's little overnight case in the other. Tamara and Dana had so lovingly packed a few changes of clothes, pajamas, comb and toothbrush, and "Boo-key," his bedtime buddy, teddy bear. He probably would be too embarrassed to sleep with him, but at least he could reach in and caress him if needed.

Tamara had gotten up early this morning and stood in the doorway with Dana waving. Neither trusted their emotions, and didn't want to break down and cry in front of Derek at the bus loading. Derek couldn't see their tears, only the waves and pasted-on-smiles. The door of the bus closed, the bus edged forward, and Derek was on his way to walking (or riding) through a new life's door.

Dana's days were more meaningful again, and even though each day brought new challenges, she had renewed her energy to meet them. Her days ere busy what with helping with the house and farm chores, cooking and learning to bake bread, and playing and tending to the children when Tamara worked or slept. Dana's small pension and dwindling savings added to Tamara's weekly paycheck along with vegetables and eggs Devon sold to neighbors enabled them to actually exist from month to month. No farm mortgage payments certainly helped.

It had only been two days since they'd bid the schoolboy goodbye, but what a difference it was making in the Barton household. Joy Dean was bored and wanted their attention constantly. The bedtime stories and romps received only half-hearted interest from all the participants. They were all counting time 'til Friday and the sight of that big, yellow school bus. Dana decided to go in the next day for her home tutor test... just in case.

Tamara was sleeping though not really restfully. She disliked working and being away from home and she worried about her boy. What was he feeling, doing, did he miss them as much as they did him?

Dana and Devon had just finished breakfast and sent Joy Dean out to gather eggs, mainly to give her something to do to quiet her nagging to go to school with Derek. Devon walked over and turned on the little kitchen television to catch the news before going out to do chores. Dana began to clear the table when the newscaster's comments caught her attention. She picked up the coffee pot, poured her son and herself another cup, and settled back into the chair she'd just risen from. They were discussing some new governmental project that was supposed to improve the present monetary system and alleviate the rampart crime element in their present society. It was sure to benefit the "shaky" economy. "At least they are recognizing that our economy is "shaky," Devon commented.

Dana leaned forward to listen a little more intently. Seemed to her that this was more than just a local or even a Federal project...this sounded to be a global plan. The discussion monopolized the television most of the day, and even when Tamara got up about noon, it was reiterating the same message. Tamara found her husband and mother-in-law glued to the TV set, and breakfast dishes still on the table. Joy Dean was sitting cross-legged on the floor watching even though she had no idea of what.

Tamara poured herself a lukewarm cup of coffee and joined the family at the table to see what was so interesting. She soon reacted in an almost hysterical manner. Her early religious teaching clicked a fear-memory in her brain. She recalled the teachings of something similar. It was something about a mark placed on the forehead and hand; she thought they called it "the Mark of the Beast." "Oh, no!" she screamed. "It's here, now we will all be damned or doomed!" She got the family's attention. Tamara never raised her voice or screamed. Devon rushed over to his wife and tried to calm her, but to no avail. She kept moaning and crying, "This is the end, this is the end." She became so upset, she had to call in sick from work, and that was a first for her.

For the next couple of weeks, the new monetary issue was the topic of conversation at dinner tables, city halls, churches, shopping centers, TV and radio, newspapers and magazines, and every couple of days letters of information came in the mail.

The government for the most part was doing a great selling job to the public. They were so convincing of all the advantages to implementing this ID implant. What they were not sharing with any but "the elect global fathers" was the other uses of the IDI. The forehead implant was explained as a backup or reserve. Besides, it was explained that some microwire extensions allowed the chip to draw energy from neuron activity in the brain and acted as a booster battery. Truth? Somewhat. It also performed as tiny transmitters sending emotional brain waves to computer scanners. "Big Brother" could scan and read emotional stability and character strengths and weakness. This helped separate the highly potential from the average or even the non-societal discardables. They could use the implant as a means to eliminate the non-productive. Earth's population was definitely overloaded and needed attention as much if not more than the monetary issue. There would just be a lot of heart attacks that would be blamed on stress or whatever. The little chip could trigger the heart rhythm if so directed. Also, every hundredth implant or even the productive beings would have a "timer" to interrupt the heart's function at the "host's" sixty-fifth year. There were too many healthy, retired people draining the usable resources of Earth. This would benefit the World's economy immensely. It would be years later before the World citizens began to question this outbreak of heart attacks. In fact, the remaining family members of those healthy, just sixty-five year old heart attack victims finally discovered the truth. But that's a later happening.

It was finally Friday, and the Barton household was preparing for a welcome home party. The clock seemed to be holding on to each minute for an hour.

Dana had gone into City Hall that morning to take the home tutor test. If she passed it, and she felt confident, she would get her certificate in a week. Then she could tutor both the children at home. Tamara just couldn't stand letting Derek leave home again; she was petrified over the news of the impending implant. She vowed she'd die first before receiving the implant. She really believed this was the "last days." She hated leaving her family to go to work, and she wouldn't let them leave the farm. So Derek's school days were put on hold.

No time for worried faces now, though. The clock on the wall said "Time!" They all grouped themselves on the front porch and strained their eyes down the road for sight of the yellow bus. "There it comes!" shouted Joy Dean. It came closer and closer, and finally came to a screeching halt. The door slid open and Derek stepped out. They all gasped for joy. He appeared older; how ridiculous, he'd only been gone a week...not the decade it had seemed!

What a homecoming! Derek couldn't stop talking; Joy Dean couldn't stop hanging on him; Tamara couldn't stop crying; Devon couldn't stop asking questions; and, Dana couldn't stop her proud, pounding heart from beating so loud she could hear no other sound!

5

A Mark of Time

DANA HAD JUST RECEIVED her first notice to report to the hospital for her IDI. She knew she would receive two more, and decides for Tamara's sake to postpone for a while. She tries to condition Tamara to "what is." "If you live in fearful expectancy, life will be sure to provide you the materialization of your fears. Your Bible says in Job 18 'to go in peace, for the journey you are on is under the eyes of the Lord.' So, if we are to trust this, how can we not also know that our paths are already laid out by a loving Creator?

If all things are ordered for our good as also stated in the Bible, then why would He deliberately arrange some centuries before a challenge so cruel as to either doom or damn His children for a decision they would have to make? He commanded us to love one another. Why? Was it just so we would have to decide between the bonds of love for our family or the fear bonds of a God who would eternally damn us for loving them too much? Tamara, my God is perfect love, and perfect love casts out all fear. Love never faileth. So I can in perfect peace give unto Caesar that which is Caesar's, and to God that which is God's. I can give my flesh to the government for the implant for that is not eternal. I give my Soul and heart filled with love to God, for that is my eternalness."

Almost, Tamara seemed convinced to Dana's reasoning. Her heart seemed to be in agreement, but old fear tapes played in her head. "But what if I would be damning myself? I can't take that chance, I just can't!" she sobbed.

A few days later, Devon and Tamara received their first notice. The children didn't understand what was happening. They just knew the adults were always discussing this "thing" that was about to happen, and Mama was crying every time they talked about it. She always hugged and cried a lot before going to work at night. This made the children uneasy although they didn't understand their mother's concern.

Devon was afraid he couldn't convince Tamara to consent to the implantation, and without it, she would probably not be able to work. He contemplated the possibilities of them making it on just his and his mom's government delegated credits they would receive. Besides, he would be drawing extra for the two children. Perhaps they could just make it if they all cut back just a little. He also wondered if Tamara's declining the program would be less noticeable if she was not working and in the public's eye. He knew how much she dreaded going to work these days, anyway, and decided it was time to present these ideas to Tamara. When he asked her to come sit on the front porch with him to listen to his ideas about her quitting work, she eagerly accepted.

Devon explained to his wife how they were all just trying very hard to make decisions that would most benefit their little family unit and enable it to survive these trying times. One thing that would help would be for Tamara to be home evenings with the family so they wouldn't worry about her. The kids needed her there then too as they were having difficulty sleeping. Tamara felt such relief over the prospects of being able to quit work and rejoin her family full time. She agreed to give her week's notice the next day.

While Tamara was still feeling elated over quitting work, Devon snuck in the rest of his planned talk. "Tamara, I know how you feel about receiving the IDI and I respect that. Our family will not be able to survive though without being able to receive the promised living credits, and I am responsible for my family's wellbeing. I think with Mom's and my IDI allotments, we could still get through this challenge. Without, we will die, maybe before the kids, maybe after seeing them die; but dying is inevitable! So Mom and I will be receiving our IDI and we will discuss this subject no further. Now, let's plan for your last day at work party. It will be so good to have you climb into bed with me again after our bedtime romp with the kids like we used to. I've sure missed you, my girl!"

Devon drove his mother to the hospital for her implant, as they were not real sure how major this procedure would be. Besides, he was there for support. The attendant in white had handed them quite a lengthy questionnaire to complete about a lot of personal information. The woman in the white uniform was not really unfriendly, but she'd sure never win the "Miss Congeniality" contest! She was attempting to assure them that this was a very simple procedure. Dana would receive a light anesthesia and while dozing, the implants would be secured. They would not even leave a scar, as the incision would be so minute.

Devon watched the attendant and his mom walk down the hallway and disappear into a surgical room. Twenty-five minutes later his mother returned to the waiting room looking the same as when he'd brought her in. Three days later, Dana waited in the waiting room for Devon. Now they were the official "saviors" of the family or among the number of the damned. Regardless, they felt very comfortable thanking "their God" for the strength and courage to complete this not chosen task.

Tamara prayed earnestly for God to have mercy and forgive her husband and mother-in-law. Yet, today she was concentrating more on her own feelings. Tomorrow was her last day at work, and she couldn't squelch this "high" she was feeling as she began to clean up before closing. If only that group at the far end of the diner would just leave, she could be on her way. Around the table sat three boisterous young men just out of their teens. Tamara had reminded them several times that it was closing time, but they only made her more annoyed with their responses. "Yah, were just waiting around to see that a good-looking girl like you gets home safe," one commented. The other two chimed in with "We are volunteering for that job, aren't you the lucky one?!"

Tamara wondered if she should call Devon, but if he would come barging in as her angry protector, they might accept the challenge and gang up on him. That could turn into a disaster. She thought of calling the police, but they had such large areas to cover; it could be an hour or longer wait in getting them there. She had to do something, so she stepped inside the manager's office to use the phone out of their sight. Just then, she saw the three get up, throw some bills on the table, and leave without so much as a backward glance. She saw them drive on down the road.

Tamara was still feeling a little uneasy as she turned off the inside lights of the café, walked through the empty lot to her car, climbed in and started it. She felt better after a couple of minutes of driving. She even began to think about only one more drive home. She was so deep in thought she didn't even notice the fast-approaching headlights of an upcoming car behind her. Not until its loud horn jolted her back into reality. It kept beeping as it pulled to her side for a short distance, and then zoomed in front of her, slowing down quickly. She was sure it was the same car as at the restaurant and it appeared to have three passengers in it, the best she could see. Tamara began to slow down too and tried to edge over into the other lane to pass. She felt her hands gripping the steering wheel with such pressure they were going numb on her. Every time Tamara would start to get into the passing lane, the other car would block her efforts. She was really feeling terror clear to the pit of her stomach.

The other car finally pulled into the oncoming lane as if to tempt Tamara into a race. She decided this may be her only chance, and to go for it. As they began to edge the speedometer up past 85 mph, the other car began crowding her over to the edge of the highway. She felt gravel under the wheels of her car and it began to be unmanageable. Suddenly, the other car began beeping loudly and moved far over into the outer lane, leaving her lane open. She tried desperately to pull her vehicle off the gravel and on to the hard cement surface, but her tires were doing a crazy dance of their own making. Then, Tamara gasped, "Oh, God!" as the realization of the impending impact hit her just before the car hit the concrete embankment of the bridge.

The next noise piercing the silence of the night was the bonding of metal and concrete creating this grotesque, accordion-shaped mass. Tamara's unconscious, bleeding head lay on her vehicle's horn, trumpeting her demise to the sleeping world.

The sheriff was heading home as his shift was over. As he eared the bridge, he heard this continual horn blasting, but could see no car lights. He rolled his window down, slowed up, and peered into the darkness from where the sound seemed to be coming. Then, he saw the mangled shape.

He had known Devon for a few years as they'd been almost neighbors, and he'd even stopped in the restaurant occasionally for coffee on his shift. Now, he had the duty to inform Devon of his wife's fatal accident.

It was a not quite cold autumn day, but at least the sun was shining. The children were bundled warm enough to keep the chill away from them, and yet their small frames were shivering. This was probably more related to their still confused emotional state than the weather. They had just recently, happily kissed and hugged their mother goodbye with the thought that in one more day they wouldn't ever have to again. Now they were telling their mama goodbye for the last time.

There was quite a gathering of friends at the little country cemetery. Tamara had endeared herself to a lot of people, and she would certainly be missed. Devon felt this more than anyone. He also felt confused, what had happened to cause this final separation from his adored life partner. The sheriff had hinted to some tire skid marks on the bridge that seemed to hint at another car perhaps being present during the accident. Beyond that, there were no clues. No matter, on the "eve" of Devon getting "his girl" back on a full-time basis, he'd lost her forever. Anger, sorrow, guilt, disbelief, and a multitude of emotions were taking their toll, and Devon suddenly felt very tired. He picked Joy Dean up, and Dana held Derek's hand as the now four-member Barton family unit walked back to the car. They loaded in and Devon looked back once more at that space of ground where Tamara would soon be resting in. He suddenly recalled a statement Tamara recently made…"I'll die before I have the ID implanted in my hand or forehead!" "Is that what had really happened, Tamara? Did you decide this was your only viable solution to this most fearful problem? Devon pondered as his eyes misted over. I think I understand the "why" now, it was your way of taking care of yourself and still being able to watch over us without guilt. Please let me feel your loving presence often though, I feel so alone here on Earth without you. Good night, my Love. Rest in peace!"

Devon brushed the moisture droplets off his cheeks, seated himself behind the steering wheel of Dana's car, and headed once again for the farm and tomorrow's new challenges.

6

New Beginnings

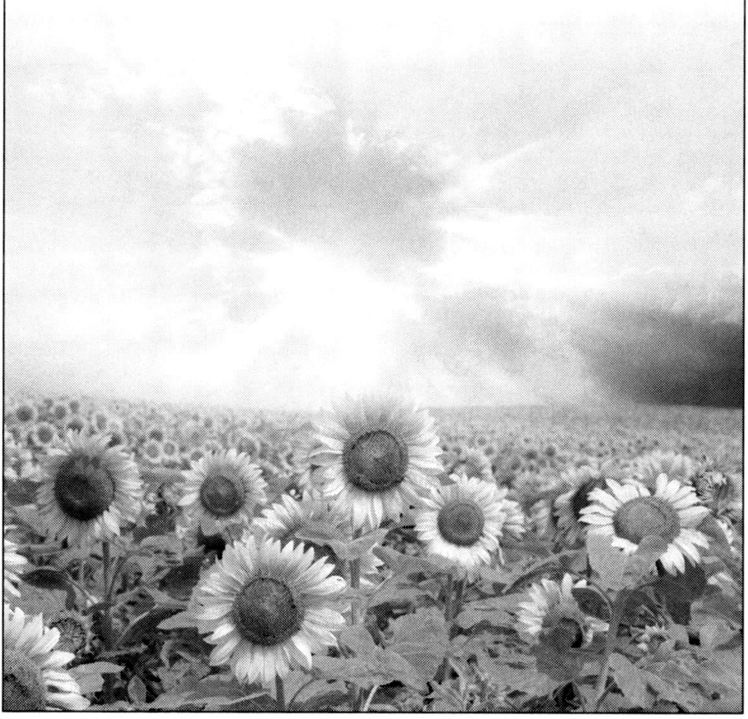

THE NEXT COUPLE OF YEARS the farm was run by robots. Slowly, life began to surge through roboticized bodies, revitalizing them with love's awakening within each sleeping heart.

Joy Dean was her daddy's constant companion. She looked more like a young Tamara each day. She had watched a program on TV where this pretty nurse had been responsible for saving a young man's life. She then had nursed him back to health. They'd fallen in love, married, and lived happily ever after. Ever since then, Joy Dean declared she would become a nurse, take care of her daddy--and when she grew up, they would marry. They'd adopt Grandma and Derek and live happily ever after. Devon would always chuckle after these declarations of love from his daughter, and perhaps they were really the needed tonic to aid his healing process.

Devon would always miss Tamara, but each day seemed easier to get involved in without feeling as if he really didn't exist. It had been like he was wearing this battery pack that allowed him to perform his daily activities; then, at night, he could turn off and sink into an exhausted oblivion.

Dana's days were busy trying to hold the family together, keeping the farm running, and finding ways to bring her family back from despair. One thing that was helping was her daily tutoring sessions with the children. Even Devon would join in and contribute his learned experience knowledge to the reservoir of wisdom being dipped into.

Joy Dean was an excellent reader, advanced for her age. She loved reading anything about health, the body, or human development."Who knows," Dana shared with her son."We might be raising a 21st century Florence Nightingale!" "She sure seems to be gifted with a soothing, healing touch when she gives those overworked muscles a rubdown," agreed Devon.

Derek...well, he was an eager student, too. His natural talents seemed to lie in mathematical computations and drawing. He was always drawing building designs, and was most particular to draw them to precise scale. Dana mused over this talent and how uncanny and advanced it was. He just had to be born for a particular mission, not yet revealed.

Then, there was the world that extended beyond their little farm retreat. It was changing also, and seemingly for the good. The Bartons had to venture out to take their extra eggs and produce to the city market so they could receive proper credit, which could be deposited into their IDI accounts. They would, in turn, pick up a few necessities that the checkout scanners would automatically deduct from their account balance. Then they would head back to the safety of the farm until the next market trip.

Even Devon had to admit, at least during his rare conversational moments, that the IDI program appeared to be working. The crime element had been drastically curtailed, and welfare was all but a forgotten program. Those who worked earned spendable credits, and those who didn't had better either be underage or disabled with an IDI sponsor—or they couldn't exist. Mothers of underage children were also exempt from work if desired. They would be eligible for extra credits for these dependents. This only applied if the pregnancies were by legal IDI participants. There was now also a three-child limit on all newly formed family units with credit penalties for non-compliance. With more people on an earning status instead of "handout" basis, more jobs were being formed to accommodate the increased labor supply. As new jobs were formed, more available credits were being accrued and being fed back into the economy as workers dared to spend again.

Even the home market was rising off its deathbed and gaining strength. Why, even Devon's neighbor, the Sheriff, had a son that had just married and wanted to build a small home on his father's land. Devon was offered the job. He was so excited as he pulled out the old carpenter's chest he'd hid back in the corner of the barn. He reached in and lovingly removed and cleaned each tool. Perhaps, he thought, there was still some living to do.

Even countries were no longer as competitive now that there was a global exchange. They had also formed a Global Council to implement and control this newly formed Universal Monetary Exchange. They had also formed a World Police Corp to make sure this system was complied with, and not misused. It also acted as a global army to arbitrate territorial disputes and to coerce non-compliant countries into submission to the Council's will.

So, it really was becoming the best of all times! People were not afraid to venture out at night. They had extra credits to indulge in the various channels of arts and entertainment. They also had more recreational time and more enticing ways to use it.

Public schools had died during the transition stage. Now most homes were purchasing home computers for educational enrichment. It was so much more convenient and actually seemed to accelerate the learning process. Students were advancing at their own speed and quickly channeled into their own unique specialty areas instead of wasting time on needless courses. Devon was very impressed with how the children were adapting to their newly acquired electronic tutor. Dana was secretly jealous of the machine. She always prided herself on her tutoring abilities, and was feeling somewhat "replaced." The children sensed this and would always ask her questions to which they already knew the answers. Then, they would look astonished that Dana knew so much.

Both the children were very special to both Dana and Devon. Yet, Joy Dean still felt it her responsibility to look after her dad; and her dad adored her for it. Derek—well...Dana never wanted to admit it to herself, but Derek just always had held a little priority standing in her heart. She felt such a bonding with him; perhaps they had earned that special closeness in another lifetime, she thought. At least she was sure that he would leave a large imprint on the world this lifetime!

Devon was beginning to awake with enthusiasm each morning. He was not only building the new house for Jason, the Sheriff's son, but also doing a lot of remodeling and enlarging around the farm.

He needed another pole barn to store the cut up wood from his place that he cut and stored in the fall to sell in the winter. He was enlarging his chicken house and was also now adding a hatchery. His chicken and egg business was accruing a lot of credits for them at the market. He had also made a root cellar and lined it with shelves to store both the fresh and the canned garden produce for family use. They still had abundant vegetables, fruits, and nuts to take to the market.

Cars were changing quickly also, not only in design, but also in how they were powered. A lot of solar and high mileage compacts were now seen on the road. All were very environmentally conscious. Gas was quite price obtainable, and there was talk of gasless vehicles on the drawing board.

Homes were being introduced to nuclear heating elements that were not only cleaner and safer, but also a lot more economical.

Churches were not very crowded these days. Most people had lost faith with organized religion. There was a real consciousness awareness sweeping the world's people. People were speaking of their spirituality much like they would discuss any other faucets of their life. People were becoming more accepting of each other's uniqueness and regarded themselves more as Earthlings than Americans, Europeans, or etc. They, too, were becoming more self-responsible, thinking individuals. If things were not to their liking, they had to own up to their part in creating it. Maybe they had not only created the mess of a few years ago, but were responsible for the better reality they were enjoying now. Perhaps, if they improved their creative skills, they could even create the Biblical mentioned “Golden Age.” Dana remembered part of a verse from the Bible that went something like . . . “as a man thinketh, so it is.”

7

Strange Winds A-Blowin'

IN THE LITTLE TWO-BEDROOM trailer down by the pond, John was just climbing out of bed. Amy, his wife, had just made a fresh pot of coffee and the aroma had drifted through the open door of the bedroom, drawing John up to meet this new day. Cameron, their 14-year-old son, was already up and out feeding the farm animals. He really loved life on the farm, and part of this attraction was Joy Dean, who even at age 12 was becoming a dark-haired beauty.

The past few years that John and Amy had lived on the farm, they had earned the friendship and gratitude of Devon and his family. Devon could never have continued his carpentry pursuits if John and Cameron had not almost completely taken over the farm labors. Amy had helped Dana a lot with the garden, and with the marketing, storing and preserving the produce. They had become close friends in spite of age differences. Amy sometimes related to Dana as the mother she'd never had. Her mother died when she was only five.

These two families had bonded into an understood partnership. They just both knew this was going to be a long-term relationship and needed no legal paperwork to bind either of them to any court-validated contract. Devon, with John and Cameron's help, was building a new three-bedroom home where the other trailer had sat. John's trailer was old and not in the best shape. They were looking forward to moving into this new home, and having the old trailer hauled off. In a few more months, if the weather held, they could realize this dream.

Meg and Don Long had lived in the other trailer. Don was a healthy, robust, 63-year-old when they first came to the farm. He was a good worker. Meg was ten years younger than Don, but a frail woman. Don had thought the country air would be good for her. It was so unbelievable to all of the farm residents when Don had an unexpected heart attack, and right on the day of his 65th birthday. He'd never had any problems with his heart before. Their son came up from the southern part of the state and arranged for the trailer to be towed down close to where he lived. He felt he needed to look after his mother now. They had not been on the farm long, but left a vacancy of more than just the space where the trailer had been.

Dana always seemed to have an inner sense about things, and even though the farm was producing in a bountiful manner, she felt a little uneasiness. She shared this feeling with Devon and John. She felt they should become even more independent and survival-ready as a precaution. She convinced them to put in a windmill for a water supply along with a couple "big man" generators for power failures. They both agreed that would be a good precautionary measure and implemented her idea immediately. Devon trusted his mother's intuitive nature. The women began to do a lot more canning, smoking meats, and storing supplies in the freezer and root cellar. They truly were becoming quite a self-sufficient little commune. They were also finding time to socialize and enjoy each other's company. They were quite a happy and contented group.

The larger cities were going through rapid changes also. No individual stores anymore. They had been replaced with sprawling malls that were so huge they had people movers to transport customers around. They were plastic benches that moved on conveyer belts and even up and down floors on escalators. They had parking garages, but most parked at the edge of the city and rode monorails to wherever they desired to go in the inner city.

Inside the malls and throughout the city, entertainment centers were located. They included virtual reality theatres. These were used a lot by people that either didn't have the time or credits to travel or do vacations. Also, with the fear of AIDS and other sexual diseases still very much rampant in the society, this provided a safe, sexual release.

Also, at various locations throughout the city, there were specialized libraries housing learning chambers. For so many predetermined credits, one could get a computerized education and degree. Universities and colleges had proven too costly to operate. This was not only more economical, but students could advance at their desired rate and be able to achieve their career goals much quicker. Derek had planned to begin his Drafting and Mechanical Drawing studies by the end of the year.

Two more years had zoomed by, Dana mused to herself. Her family was certainly outgrowing their childhood. She was also feeling very uneasy about her family planning her birthday party tomorrow. She would be 65. Not that she felt fearful over it, but, not only Don but several other healthy community citizens had mysteriously died with heart attacks at that same age. Was it just coincidence? she wondered. No time to give it more thought. Besides, other than leaving her family, death had never been a frightening thought. Not living her life to the fullest was her real fear.

Joy Dean had started attending the Nursing Learning Center. She had always been the compassionate caretaker, especially of her father. It was only natural for her to pursue a nursing career. She seemed to have a gift of healing in her hands, and people always remarked that her rubdowns always made them feel better.

Cameron was attending the Learning Center, too, along with taking over more and more of the farm's responsibilities. He dearly loved working the land and caring for the animals. He was taking courses in Agriculture and Animal Husbandry. He was very muscular, though tall and lean. His sandy red hair and blue eyes made a handsome figure of a man. Joy Dean was as attracted to him as vice-versa. They were becoming more than best friends, and the families were most pleased.

Cameron and Joy Dean decided that when their educational goals were met, they would make definite wedding plans and shared the news with their parents. Devon had to mull that news around in his head for a while before he could join in the festive mood of the others. He sure liked Cameron and was glad he'd be there to take care of his girl. It was just the accepting the fact that she'd grown up on him and it was time to share her with the rest of the world.

Derek had already received his Associate's Degree and was going for his Master's. Then, he wanted to go to one of the bigger cities to pursue his architectural career. Dana was so proud of him, but very remiss about his leaving the farm. What if she should have a heart attack and not get to say her goodbyes to him?

That fall was unusual in that every few days they would have a fierce windstorm. It was good that they had the windmill and the generators, as there were a number of power outages that caused extreme difficulties for a lot of people.

Then, hurricane Ida came for a visit, and stayed, and stayed. It had come into the Gulf and headed for the Panhandle—only there it stalled for over a week. The winds and rains were devastating. Finally, it edged across Georgia and out into the Atlantic. It was not through with its Florida visit yet. It had weakened considerably, but had enough strength to slide down the coast to the Cape, then veered inland until it exited out into Tampa Bay and into the warm Gulf waters again. This time it picked up strength and headed back up its old route to the Panhandle. The already flooded lowlands gave way to the storm's vindictiveness this time. The Okefenokee Swamps became so oversaturated it began sinking, and from Apalachee Bay in Florida to St. Simons Island in Georgia, a new inter-ocean channel was formed. Florida had become an island disconnected from the mainland. All this happened in the matter of a day's time. Ida exhausted herself in the Atlantic, but left her mark for all time.

The casualty toll mounted daily and the devastation was unbelievable. People panicked; riots were commonplace. Once again people began to talk about "end time" predictions. The farm had received a lot of rain and wind damage, but not the destruction of elsewhere. The crops were gone and some roof damage. Other than that, they felt very blessed. The generators and windmill were providing them with fresh water. The root cellar and smokehouse were their store. Dana had survived her 65th birthday, and now Ida. She knew there was a Divine Plan for her and her family unit. Whatever was ahead, they would be fine. Now was the time for them to reach out and share with their less fortunate neighbors. Perhaps if there was any good to be gained from this period of time, it could be the coming together without differences. It was no longer a time for "going it alone;" it would have to become a wholeness or nor nothing.

8

The Dark Prince

IN A RURAL SWITZERLAND community, not too many kilometers from Geneva, is a most unusual estate. The dwelling resembled an ancient, Egyptian pyramid. On the massive stone entrance was carved the words of an Egyptologist: "Of course the holes are not for you to look in, but for the Pharaoh to look out . . . perhaps at the stars in the Northern Sky called the Imperishables because they never set." There was an electronic force field surrounding the lush, garden landscape that extended for a 20-acre radius around the pyramid. There was a helicopter port in the back to transport him to his computer parts factory in Munich, Germany, or to any other desired destination.

The owner of this estate was said to be a computer genius, and one of the wealthiest men in all Europe, possibly America. Though uninvited guests were never allowed on the premises, the help had told stories about everything in the living structure and the yards were controlled and operated from a main computer within the pyramid.

The few known witnesses to have seen him described him as a very athletic, well-preserved, 50-some-year-old man. In truth, he was triple that estimate. His name was Epsolum Petra. He was destined to play a large role in this particular Earth-time.

He had studied all the Earth's known religions, and though well versed, he felt to adopt any would be to demean his own superior reasoning. He did recognize the incarnate abilities of the astral body and could give an accurate accounting of several of his physical embodiment returns.

One of the earliest Earth's residences was as Luxor, whose temples still preside over the busiest tourist centers in southern Egypt (Thebes, Waset). A grand avenue lined with sphinxes once linked the temple—built by Amenhotep III sometime around mid-1300 B.C., and enlarged by Tutankhamen, Ramses II, and Alexander the Great—to Karnal. Alexander was another of his physical embodiments along with Herod, King of Judea, and Napoleon Bonaparte. He was very comfortable with power and knew well how to use it.

He really felt a concern for the economic state of affairs the world was experiencing. Also the degeneration of society's values needed to be addressed. He felt he could "make the difference." He saw himself as "the man of the hour" and Earth time fast running out.

He was aware of human's mind abilities to extend beyond the physical world into the realm of human energy waves. He knew the body was much more than a magnificent machine. He recognized the inter-relatedness of mind, emotions, health and disease. Control people's mental activity, and you control their physical activity. You could spur creativeness or deaden desires. Minds could be so opened that deceit and crime could no longer be concealed. Mind conversations could become as plausible as computer inter-netting. Evil forces could be checked and held in abeyance while potentials could be urged to attain their highest aspirations.

Within the walls of the pyramid, the man gives birth to a program that will alleviate his world of its undesirables, create a new world monetary system that will save a collapsing economy, and form a workable global government. He also sees himself as the recognized leader of this world government.

He is pleased with his new program, and calls a summit meeting of the world leaders to neutral Geneva to introduce it to them. A new World Council is formed.

Since this was to be a computer controlled and enforced program, they decide to house the main, base computer named

"Mother" at the Council Building in Geneva. It is housed in a well-guarded, restricted, underground vault room. Since "Father Petra" would be the sole programmer and only one to access this chamber, it also was provided with comfortable living quarters and survival needs for as long a period as was deemed necessary by Epsolum.

He explained the ID implant and how it would ease so many of the world's problems. He felt the need to not include the total program and so withheld important details, even from his trusted Council members. He feared they would veto the whole package thinking he had gone too far playing God. Besides, they were not of the same high caliber of intelligence or awareness, he reasoned to himself.

The Council had no trouble convincing the world leaders to implement this new concept of the IDI or of the need for a global police force to regulate and enforce this program.

Epsolum was viewed by many as a "savior," but others not so receptive wondered if he might be the "Anti-Christ." Perhaps, if they had been more completely informed of the rest of his program already within "Mother's Memory," they'd have proclaimed him the "Dark Prince!"

"Mother" and the IDIs were transmitting a lot more than banking credits. The little micro wires had a big job. They informed "Mother" of each wearer's potentials, submissiveness, their value to the system, and personal beliefs. Those deemed worthy would be given priority health care credits and living credits. Others seen as non-profitable could be programmed for cell degeneration or immune deficiency processing to be activated in the host's body. Others would have a fatal heart attack or be denied access to living credits. The possibilities would have programmed extended life patterns sent to their DNA. Even those who'd been preselected to depart at age 65 could be reprogrammed by "Mother." Just as easily, a non-game player could be terminated at any time by apparent natural causes. Even the "chosen" Council received subtle clues that they had perhaps better not question "the programmer," as they also had IDIs.

Of course, the IDI chips were to be manufactured at Epsolum's factory in Munich. They were called the "Omega Chip" because:

"O" for organic . . . of or affecting an organ of the body.

"M" for magnetic . . . a condition of space established by the presence of an electric current.

"E" for electroencephalograph . . . an instrument that records the electrical activity of the brain.

"G" for galvanometer . . . a device for detecting or measuring small electric currents by means of mechanical effects produced by the current to be measured.

"A" for acetylcholine . . . a white crystalline compound (C7H16NO2) that transmits nerve impulses across intercellular gaps.

Yes, truly this man would alter history; his world would never be the same again. Epsolum was definitely feeling his new power surging through his veins and he felt as immortal as the stars in the Northern Sky saw through his ceiling portal of his pyramid home. The stars sent him a message also . . . even their brilliance would burn out and cease in time. "Only the creations of the Omnipotent Creator were eternal!" the heavens declared.

9

Together, We Stand

FLORIDA WAS LIKE A SMALL CHILD that had gotten lost from its mother at a big mall. Life had become so fearful and bewildering again for Floridians. They were at a loss as to how to survive alone without being attached to "Mother America." They had always depended on tourism, and other than the ones caught here after Ida had destroyed northbound highways, the tourist door had been closed. Florida also depended on the trains and trucks for manufactured goods and building supplies. These now had to either be flown in or arrive at coastal seaports. Florida felt orphaned and abandoned.

The worst was the vagueness of news trickling back as to the extent of Ida's damage. Aid was being flown in to the survivors. The number of unfortunate victims that had been swept away by floodwaters to the Gulf or Atlantic had been impossible to tabulate. Mass graves had become a necessity for the other fatalities. There was not much cleanup as destroyed buildings, vehicles and such had sunk or swept out to sea.

Inland Florida was suffering also. Panic was turning hard working or fairly responsible citizens into survivalists at all costs. There was rioting and robbing along with physical violence in most of the cities. Rural communities were faring somewhat better, but were afraid to venture out beyond the safety of their homes. No one trusted anyone, and they certainly lost faith in the government to protect or provide for them. Water and electricity were still provided services in most areas, but gas and propane were scarce and hard to come by. Besides, truck drivers and deliverymen were constantly being hijacked for their goods and vehicles, and refused to be on the roads.

The farm was in much better shape than most with their stored food supplies, wood for fuel, milk and eggs, meat and fish from the pond, and fresh water because of the windmill. They were grateful they didn't have to venture out into the present chaotic world.

Devon and John worked from before sunup to well past sundown each day repairing and caring for the farm and helping their neighbors to regain some sense of pre-Ida living. Dana and Amy made sure their neighbors had food enough to get by and Cameron and Derek would deliver the "care packages."

Joy Dean would often ride with them to care for a sick child, set a broken limb, and even deliver a few babies. Her nursing courses were sure coming in handy, but then she'd always seemed to have a natural healing touch, too. The neighbors began to refer and call the house asking for "Doc" Joy.

Cameron had located and gotten permission to use a large, vacant but sturdy church. He had made it into a Community Meeting Hall and Storehouse. Everyone brought in any "extras" such as clothes, blankets, food supplies (fresh and canned), tools, books, and even games and toys. Community members could take whatever they needed, never more. In return, they would leave some articles for another neighbor. No exchange of credits, just neighborly exchange of love. They also had a bulletin board with "help needed" requests and a "help available section.

Each Saturday evening after chores, a community-formed band would meet at the Hall and enliven the air with music. Couples danced, socialized, and bonded with each other. It was a very healing event.

Sunday afternoons they'd gather at the churchyard and bring blankets or lawn chairs. This was the adult's sharing time. They shared hopes and dreams, heartaches and disappointments, or just new ideas to improve the living in their little neighborhood. The children took this time to remember to be kids again. They invented new games and replayed old favorites. In season, they would have a corn husking bee, a barbecue, or a watermelon feast. The women even revived the old "quilting bees" and created masterpieces.

They were really becoming a self-sufficient municipality. Things were not that good elsewhere, but news of their "commune" success was spreading to other rural areas. Also, people began to leave the big cities and congregate in similar communities throughout the countryside. Florida was becoming "urbanized!"

One evening, just about dusk, Devon and his extended family were enjoying the day's closing in the peaceful outdoors. As they sat communing with nature and each other, they noticed this manly figure approaching them. He was only half way up their long driveway, but they were sure he was not one of their locals. Who could this stranger without a vehicle be, and what was he wanting from them, they were all thinking. Devon arose from his chair and started to walk towards him. He just didn't want an unknown too close to his family without first "checking him out." John and the boys got up from their chairs and followed behind Devon. The stranger must have wondered if this was a cordial advancement or a threatening one. "Howdy," Devon greeted, then paused to evaluate the stranger's reaction and response.

The stranger soon assured the menfolk his only intention was to ask for a drink of water and to sit a spell to rest his tired body. He'd started out from the north side of Ocala yesterday driving down to Sebring to check on his aged mother. He'd stopped at a fruit stand just about 20 miles back to get something to eat on the way down and to take to his mother. While he was getting his produce, his car was hot-wired and stolen. It was such a common occurrence that police would not even make reports. He had started walking in hopes of catching a ride. "There just is not that many cars on the road these days, and the ones out are afraid to pick up strangers." The stranger went on to tell how he'd slept in this big culvert last night and that was why he looked so dirty and disheveled. He had at least had the fruit to eat. It just was so hot and he was so thirsty he reasoned away his fears and decided to brave coming up to ask for a drink.

Dana was already pouring him a fresh glass of the lemonade they'd all been enjoying and motioned him to sit in her chair. She informed the stranger they had just finished supper and was going to warm him up a plate. She was not sure why, but she felt instantly drawn to this man. She remembered the story from Sunday school about the "Good Samaritan" and somehow she felt comfortable giving hospitality to this being. She scurried off into the kitchen with Amy right behind her, cautioning her to be careful. "We don't really know this person or what he really wants from us, you know." "It's okay," Dana assured her friend, "I feel it inside."

The stranger not only cleaned the last morsel of food off the plate, but also downed three glasses of lemonade. Then, right in the middle of conversations, dropped off to sleep in the lawn chair. They had a family conference and decided to put a camping cot up in the tack room of the barn. The room had a little half-bath facility and was clean and dry. The stranger could rest there. Maybe he could work around the farm for a couple of days and then go to Sunday's get together. Someone may know of a ride going in the direction of Sebring. They woke the stranger and informed him of their plan. He said he was most grateful for their kindness and that their goodness would be rewarded.

The family members had mixed emotions about their guest, and yet each felt this was an unusual person who would somehow affect the life of each of them. It was like a messenger sent to give them each special inspiration. For now, it had been a long day; morning would greet them all too soon. They said their goodnights to each other, and the darkness erased the challenges of the day.

10
The Messenger

GABRIEL NEWMAN WAS AWAKE and silently meditating. He was very grateful for this comfortable bed and quiet tack room. He knew that his stopover was not by chance, but then he recognized that nothing was by chance. He had felt very blessed to have been introduced to his own spirituality, and tried to live his life as the Spirit directed. Gabriel knew it had guided him to these special people and hoped he would be for them whatever he needed to be.

He heard the barn door open and lights flooded the dark barn. Gabe opened the tack room door and was greeted by John. "Good morning. I'm sorry if I woke you," apologized John. John was still not sure this guest was totally trustworthy. Though he often started his farm chores this early, this morning he was somewhat edged on by curiosity. He wished to find out more about the stranger.

Gabe walked over and started to pitch clean straw into each cow's stall right along with John without hesitation. Neither spoke until John had let the cows in from the outside corral and locked them in to their individual areas. Gabe then joined in the feeding ritual, one big can of oats for each cow. Only after the milking machine was humming away did John wander over to Gabe's vicinity and began the nonchalant interrogation. "You got family in Ocala?" "No, my mother and I are all that's left of my family," Gabe informed him. "You have a business or work there?" Gabe, realizing John's motive for questioning was harmless and just protective of his family, offered to share his life's story with his inquisitive coworker.

Gabe told him how he'd been born and raised in Tallahassee, the only child of Bob and Ruth Newman. His dad was a truck driver and would often take Gabe along on his cross-country trips. Gabe loved these road adventures and relished sharing private time with his dad.

Even after starting Junior College, he'd occasionally slip a trip or two in on his breaks. Then, that devastating day they received news from a hospital chaplain in Des Moines, Iowa. Dad had a fatal heart attack while at a truck stop in the area.

Gabe had flown up and arranged for his dearest friend's body to be sent home for burial. He also got permission from the company to bring his father's truck back to home base. It was like a farewell trip to the son.

He became the man of the house, put his college plans on hold, used the insurance money to purchase his own truck, and became self-employed. Within five years, he had advanced his status to a small fleet of seven trucks, a wife, and an 18-month-old baby girl. They lived with Mom, who adored her new family. Life was good!

Then devastation hit again! His wife, Gina, was taking Christy, their daughter, to a doctor's appointment. The light was green as Gina followed the traffic on through without noticing the speeding car approaching her on the driver's side. It was an instantaneous transition for Gina, and their daughter joined her mommy three days later. The intoxicated teenager driving the car that hit them would probably be a lifetime paraplegic.

Gabe couldn't stay in Tallahassee any longer, and moved his trucking unit to Ocala, Florida. He was on the road constantly as a means to escape his mental monsters. His mother, who had moved there with him, became very lonesome. So when this friend from church invited her to come to Sebring and share her house, she promptly agreed.

Gabe really was not concerned with his health or safety. He thought nothing about picking up hitchhikers. He wasn't even hesitant as he pulled over and motioned to this strange to climb into his cab. He now realizes that even then, there was a plan for his life, and that nothing was by chance. He even has wondered if his passenger on that ride might not have been an angel sent by his living wife or a caring Creator.

They did very little conversing during the next couple hundred miles before the rider thanked him and asked to be let out. He did make one brief remark about how sometimes silence can be more inspirational than surface chatter; that souls could speak to each other in the quietness. He stepped out and was gone before Gabe could inform he had left a big, blue book titled *A Course In Miracles* on the seat. Inside was a note in very feminine handwriting that said: "Remember, you can overcome any obstacle, conquer any fear, and accomplish your dreams, if you just connect with 'this' Source. It has a not only kept my life in order, but helps me to be wherever I am most needed, just as you were there for me. Bless you, my friend . . . you are one of my day's many miracles!" It aroused this trucker's interest to the extent that the book was read and reread. Slowly the miracle happened in my life . . . it became life to me.

"Well, that's my story, at least up to Ida. I have seven trucks that are running the highways of the states, but can't make it home. In time, Mother and I may fly up and begin to round them up. But for now, my energies are being directed to unfinished tasks here in Florida."

John still wasn't sure why this man had been directed here, but felt it had a higher reasoning than he was presently capable of relating to.

John felt comfortable enough with the stranger to share his inner concerns with him. "You know, I've had this feeling of late that I won't be around to see my family through these difficult times." "Put that thought to rest John." Gabe patted his new friend on the back as they walked out of the barn and towards Devon's house. "You will not only be here for your present family, but will see your grandchildren playing and growing up on this very landsite." Gabe chuckled. It felt like a prediction you could bank on to John, and he needed to claim it—so he did!

As they knocked and entered the back door and into Dana's kitchen, there was a welcoming aroma of bacon, eggs and coffee. Dana was just taking hot biscuits out of the oven and motioned them to join Devon at the table. John declined, as Amy would be waiting for him to eat breakfast with his family.

Devon was already dishing up his plate. He had to get going real soon. He was helping a neighbor build some granaries. It would supply food for several of the farm's livestock during the non-pasture times. Instead of being paid for his labors, Devon and the other helpers would be receiving food for their animals as needed. Everything was on a barter system in their newly formed "commune." Credits were still used for manufactured supplies they needed from town.

Dana cleared the table and then asked Gabe if he'd like to help gather pecans this morning. He agreed, and they gathered some pails and wandered off to the pecan orchard. Dana felt very comfortable with the stranger, though she wasn't sure why. She was usually very reserved with new acquaintances, but found herself chatting away. She was verbally reminiscing on how she came to the farm, and how Tamara died leaving her to raise the children. She shared how she always felt that even during the worst of times, there was a higher order to things that would allow goodness to come from it. She was so grateful her family had been led to this farm and guided into preparing for "lean" times. Others were still going through real tribulations.

"It is because you were 'in tune' to your inner-ness," Gabe commented, and then went on to say, "You are a special person and because of your faith, you will not only be a guiding force for your family, you will also see the rewards of your labors. You will not only be a co-creator with the chosen of this time in establishing the new age, but you will actually enter the golden city . . . that is your providence."

Dana was not sure what all that meant, but it was a warming thought to hold on to. She tucked it away inside to digest later. Right now, they had to get these pails of pecans back to the barn to bag for bartering and credits.

Amy was just heading towards the hen house for the morning gathering of eggs. She eyed Dana and the stranger with their loaded pails. She feared her friend's trusting nature would surely get her into trouble one of these days. That's why she was so startled in the midst of reaching for an egg when a voice said, "Could I intrude on your space? I've never been on a farm and find its activities most interesting." Gabe was smiling and approaching hesitantly towards the uneasy egg gatherer.

Amy did not want to appear unfriendly, but neither was she stopping her chores to chat. Gabe watched awhile and then began to gather a few eggs and gently place them into Amy's basket. He felt Amy's sense of uneasiness with his presence and tried to ease it with, "You are all so blessed to be living in this special place surrounded by people and things you love and who love you. This is a comfortable and secure place to raise a family. You can feel at ease and non-fearful. Of course," he continued, "we take this same feeling of security with us no matter where our life path takes us when we realize that God is always with us. God's a mighty presence in our lives and an unlimited source of strength and courage. We can let go feelings of anxiety and trust God's perfect order to bless us in every situation." Now it was Amy who was smiling and feeling somewhat ashamed of her earlier reservations about this person. Weren't they really all children of the same Father, she thought. Dana looked out the kitchen window at the two laughing and talking and thought that was a most unusual happening she was witnessing.

Cameron had been the emergency attendant at the church switchboard when the call came in for "Doc." Jenny Blair was going into labor and needed her assistance. He called and told Joy Dean to be ready; he'd pick her up in 20 minutes. Joy Dean had just poured herself a cup of coffee to wake up. She'd been up most of the night with a sick child and had tried to sleep in hoping to recharge her overworked battery. Cameron pulled up, beeped, and then exchanged greetings with Gabe who was resting in the porch swing. "Come on and ride with us. You can see some of our neighborhood, and maybe someone over at the Blair's may know of an available ride heading towards Sebring," Cameron invited the stranger. So the three of them raced the stork to the Blair's!

Three anxious-filled hours later, the Blairs had increased in stature by nine pounds. Joy Dean had successfully delivered a healthy baby boy. She felt very good about her day as she placed the little bundle into the daddy's waiting arms.

Joy Dean was exhausted and wanted nothing more than to get home, bathe, and go back to bed. The conversation going on between Cameron and Gabe caught her attention, and she soon revived and joined in.

They were discussing "predestination" and Gabe was imparting his thoughts on the matter. "I think we have pre-chosen goals, challenges, dreams, and even redo lessons we bring with us to the physical plane. Perhaps many are carryovers from previous life experiences. I believe we even select the most conducive environment and choose that people who would be the best of all helpmates to reach those pre-birth goals. I think we have even chosen the parents that would most benefit our predestined plans. Just like you and Joy Dean's paths crossing . . . it was not by chance. You were both needed in this space and at this time to share your special talents and also to support each other's spiritual goals and growth. You both have been destined to help create a better world. You will not only help give birth to it, but nurture it into the healthy, happy world it was always meant to be."

Cameron and Joy Dean were so enthralled with the stranger's message they didn't realize they had pulled into the drive. They were still mesmerized as they pulled up to the front of the house and turned the key off. It was Devon tapping on the windshield that brought them back to reality. "Everything all right?" Devon questioned. He was concerned things had not gone well over at the Blair's.

Later that afternoon, Derek asked the stranger if he'd like to catch a few from the pond for supper. Gabe was most eager to join Derek. It had been way too long since he'd held a fishing pole in his hand. It was an ideal day to appreciate sitting on a grassy bank, feel the warm breeze fan your face, and silence broken only by a bird or a cork splashing the lazy pond's surface.

They hadn't sat for very long when Derek began talking, and talking. "Heard you've traveled to most of the states. What's it like? I've never been over 200 miles from here except when we moved from Missouri to Florida. I can't remember much of that, though. I was planning to go north after I received my Master's Degree in Drafting and Design. I had to postpone my degree because of the storms, and all. I still dream of doing this someday, but not as often. Sometimes, I almost forget what 'the dream' was. Tell me, do you think we'll ever get back to normal living again?"

Gabe waited a moment before speaking. He wanted to be sure Derek was finished. He sensed the young man had bottled up this conversation for an awfully long time and waited for just such a time to uncap it. Finally, Gabe spoke. "I'm sure some people think you are a dreamer or hint that you are something less than you should be." "Yeah, right," Derek agreed. Gabe continued, "They don't realize you are using the tools of imagination and faith, and creating a scene of good that is a real possibility for you." "Think that's how it is?" Derek asked. "Yes. You recognized your dream and it will start unfolding soon. It's okay to be a dreamer and to want to explore what God has created you for. Never let anyone, including yourself, convince you that your dreams can't come true—not when you know they come from the Divine Good just waiting for your acceptance. Your dreams will someday bless you and all those whose lives you touch." With that, Gabe pulled in his fourth fish and put it on the stringer. What a day, he thought, and what a fine bunch of new friends he'd made. He would really miss them.

Derek pulled up the stringer of seven fish. He'd been outfished, but felt most content and happy with the afternoon's excursion.

That evening, after the cornbread and fish, Devon and the stranger went out in the yard to relax. It was just about this time two days ago that Devon had extended his hand of welcome to the stranger.

He didn't seem like a stranger anymore; in fact, it seemed like they'd just renewed an old friendship. Devon mused to himself that perhaps a bond had already been formed between these two in another lifetime.

Gabe turned to Devon and, as if he'd just read his mind, said, "Thank you for your hospitality. I feel I've just dropped in for a family reunion. Your family is very special, and I will take this memory with me and treasure it as I would my own family. I feel we will have a chance to relive these moments. If not here, then in another space and time." Gabe went on addressing his friend, "You are a good man, Devon, and your goodness is the ingredient that is transforming our world. Your goodness, along with others of your nature, are the creators of the coming age. You are co-creating the new world with your goodness and God's blessing."

Since they were to have a big day tomorrow at the Community Hall, the farm residents all wandered off to their individual beds. In the quietness of the evening darkness, each reviewed the stranger's visit and their personal interactions with him. Each felt his visit was not by chance, and that somehow their lives had all been somewhat enlightened.

11

Farewells And Hellos

CARS, BIKES, AND SEVEN horse-drawn carts were finding parking sites at the Community Center. People were already finding some prime spots for their chairs and blankets. It was another one of those beautiful, early summer days that Florida is famous for.

Devon, Dana, and Derek arrived and immediately began to spread the news of the stranger. They mentioned his wanting a ride heading towards Sebring, but mainly, they shared their interesting conversations with this new friend. Amy and John had arrived shortly after, and were expounding the wisdom of the stranger also.

When Cameron and Joy Dean arrived with the stranger, the stage was set, the audience primed and ready, and the guest of honor led unsuspectingly to the big chair in the center of the forming crowd.

Devon introduced his new friend and explained again his need for transportation to Sebring. John then spoke up and urged Gabe to share how even when things were at their worst, he found the will to regain his life. He added it might encourage them, as some had really gone through some "bad" times. "Yes," Kathryn Thompson spoke up. She had recently lost her husband to a heart attack. He was only 65. "These are really scary times, some think it is the final judgment and we are all doomed."

Gabe agreed with Mrs. Thompson that these were indeed scary times, but that goodness could also be gleaned from these times. He said, "Look around at what necessity has already created right here. I understand a few years back you didn't even know the names of all your neighbors, and now you've become an extended family. You have internalized "Love your neighbor..."

Gabe paused for a while as each felt the warm feeling of friendship cloak them with a blanket of gratitude. Then he leaned forward and continued in a most reassuring voice; the children were listening, too. "I would like to share what some spiritual teachers have shared with me. They believe that time has been readjusted to help us do, together, what our separate pasts would hinder. We are going beyond fear, for no two minds can join in the desire for love without love joining them. This is the love that casts out fear."

The crowd sat silent waiting for Gabe to continue. "The Last Judgment is a most threatening thought. It is that because you don't understand it. It was brought into being after we separated from our oneness with our Creator. This separation occurred over millions of years and the Last Judgment will extend over a similarly long period, and perhaps even longer. Its length can however be greatly shortened by miracles. If a sufficient number become truly miracle minded, this process could be immeasurably shortened. It is essential, however, that we free ourselves from fear quickly, because we must emerge from the conflict if we are to abolish the fear in our brothers. When we view everything as lovable, there will be no reason for fear to remain."

"But do you think we are living in the predicted last days?" Jenny Blair questioned Gabe. "The catastrophes happening may indicate God's judgment on the earth in a negative sense. They could also be indicating a failure of all of us on earth to develop a level of awareness that could control these elements. There have always been these natural disasters and they will most likely continue and even intensify if the physical consciousness is not dominated and controlled by spiritual consciousness. I sincerely suggest that we strive for enlightenment and also to stop feeding fear energy into our world by dwelling on negative predictions."

Gabe took a long sip of lemonade from a glass Mrs. Thompson handed him and then continued, "Jesus tried to show us the power of love as the essential component in building a human world of peace. It is the only salvation for this world, at it is up to us to stop condemning our world, but through love, start to save it." "I truly believe that all over this planet small groups are being drawn together and will be taught how to survive these times and how to help others. Even more important, they are learning to share love and will send out enough positive energy to our sick world that it will respond and find a way to heal. So there is a reason for you each not only to survive, but also to prepare for whatever is needed from you at this time for your world to survive. The future is being created today in our hearts and minds." With that, Gabe walked over to the buffet table and the ladies had previously set up.

Mrs. Thompson edged her way through the crowd forming at the table and sidled in behind the stranger. She told him how much his talk had meant to her. It seemed to give her the courage to accept the changes in her life with renewed faith. She also told him that she never learned to drive ad that after her husband died, their car just sat in the garage. He could drive it to Sebring and send her whatever credits he though it was worth.

Gabe was so touched, all he could say was, “Bless you. May I leave this book as a promissory note that I will repay your kindness and soon!” He placed a very worn, blue book in her hands. She read the title. It was *A Course In Miracles.*

Gabe said his goodbyes to all his new friends, and knew he had made more than casual acquaintances the last few days. Lasting bonds had been formed.

Cameron and Joy Dean had said they would give him and Mrs. Thompson a ride to her home so he could pick up the car. Gabe gave one last goodbye to his special new friends—Devon, Dana, John and Amy. Then he paused for a moment before shaking Derek’s hand. “Go for that degree and cultivate that dream—it is almost creation time. Be ready, because sometimes the Universe only taps us on the shoulder once, and if we don’t respond, it taps another shoulder. Goodbye my fishing partner!”

Derek listened and began to prepare for that tap. He started back to the Learning Library. Life in the cities was somewhat more settled these days.

Transportation was better, too. The monorails had not only been repaired but also extended. From north of Gainesville to the fork branching toward Tampa and St. Pete, and also to Miami. Devon rode it to Orlando, which was about an hour’s ride form the farm. He was happy to be back earning his degree. Just two or three months should net Derek his degree.

Cameron and Joy Dean were traveling throughout Florida, helping to set up little rural communes like the one they had initiated. His reputation for successfully creating independent communities had spread. Even the government had heard, and was not really pleased. They began investigations to see if he was avoiding the credit plan or illegally using it. So far, they couldn't find any solid evidence, but Joy Dean was worried they would.

They decided not to chance waiting for better times to get married. Cameron and Joy Dean gathered their family together to plan a wedding.

Everyone turned out in their gala apparel that Sunday at the Community Center. Phoebe Jones played her guitar and sang some selected love songs. Derek had dressed in his best shirt and slacks, and drove the nervous groom to the Center. He was honored to be asked to be the best man. The sheriff's granddaughter was Joy Dean's bridesmaid. Joy Dean was wearing the dress her mother had been married in. Devon and Dana transported the bride. Devon looked over at his daughter in the seat beside him and whispered softly, "She looks just like you did that day, Tamara. You'd be so proud of our girl...she grew up just fine!"

It was the first wedding at the Center, and what a special one! It somehow assured them all that love would truly find a way to see them all into a better tomorrow.

The world still had to wait yet for a while for "those" better tomorrows. Three weeks after the joyous wedding, the National News Center told of the chaos that had suddenly struck the west coast.

It seemed that radon gas levels in wells along the northern margin of the Los Angeles basin had caused the San Andreas Fault to begin to split and divide. Close to a 400-some mile long stretch of California had toppled into the sea.

Before the states could begin to mentally register what had taken place on the west coast, the ground below Manhattan started to crumble, causing buildings to collapse and whole sections to be buried.

Like a runaway train catapulting over a precipice, disaster after disaster occurred. Numerous volcano eruptions in both North and South America and Hawaii caused a blocking force, keeping out the sun's rays and affecting growing seasons. This resulted in poor crops and famine conditions. Russia began to take advantage of this disabling condition and stirs up trouble. In both North and South America, people despaired... those with a lot of credits were able to make it, the poor suffered. Those in the little Florida Commune were faring fairly well for now.

There was a lot of moving going on. The Space Center at the Cape was relocating to White Sands, New Mexico. They felt the environment to be much more stable there. Thousands of west coast residents were doing an exodus inland after the big quake. The coast was scarcely populated now with only the most determined or foolish hangers on.

Also, around 250 world citizens had moved completely off Earth to the newly built space station. The International Space Station had become a reality about eight years ago. It was home to groups of scientists, engineers, astronauts, crew, staff and some family members. It always had a reserve-readied shuttle docked and two more docking stalls for incoming.

So this was a period of change on this home of human beings. It seemed as if they were learning how fast they could adapt to change and Mother Nature was their teacher. They were learning how to pull from hidden reservoirs of strength, how to rebuild destroyed dreams and even how to say goodbyes.

12
Fearful Illusions

CAMERON HAD JUST RETURNED from assisting a newly formed commune outside of Lakeland. He had been gone almost a week, but to him, it felt like a year. He hated being away from Joy Dean even for a night. She was in the last month of pregnancy, and it was a difficult time for her to travel.

Joy Dean had been taking her grandmother on all her birthing calls, and now Dana was becoming a top-notch midwife. She was still hesitant about taking over the job of delivering her own great grandchild, but that had been the main reason for the "crash course." Joy Dean knew everything would proceed exactly as the Universe had ordered. She only wished the "big day" would hurry up some.

Joy Dean informed Cameron that two state officials were out in the neighborhood asking them a lot of questions about Cameron. They all said they were really not able to offer any information as we generally kept our personal business very private. Joy Dean had felt very uneasy about this but was trying hard to camouflage these feelings from her husband. They had been forced to share so much of their alone time with others that for now, the only thing of importance was they were together...alone. Dana and Devon usually tried to give them private space during these times, and stayed busy with outside or neighborhood activities.

"Well, at least the afternoon and evening had been perfect." Joy's mind reviewed the past, happy hours of bliss and then quickly projected into a possible threatening future. She watched the blue compact pull into the drive, stop by the front gate, and two men made their way to the front door. Joy's first thought was to ignore them in hopes they would just go away. Cameron had noticed them too, and was already approaching the door. He opened it and greeted the two strangers.

"We are looking for a Mr. Cameron Townsend," the one nearest the door informed. "I'm he," Cameron proclaimed. "You need to come with us for some clarification of claims against you concerning the government." "What claims?" Joy raised her voice in nervous bewilderment. "Instigating unrest with the credit system, creating a non-authorized bartering system, and arousing false suspicions in the IDI's role causing heart attacks of supposedly healthy 65 year olds," the other man, who had now stepped inside the door, explained.

Joy felt fearful watching them drive off with Cameron even though he had tried to assure his wife he would be home in time for supper.

The three Bartons ate supper alone and wondered what was keeping Cameron. Devon called on the Tele-Com the next morning to their neighbor, the sheriff. He said he would try to check out the situation and get back to them. All the information he could get was that Cameron had been taken by air-jet to Atlanta to stand trial. Joy was devastated!

It was the only topic at Sunday's community meeting. While everyone was indignant over Cameron's arrest, there was nothing they could do to rectify it. Some even suggested that maybe they should discontinue the "Commune" activities for a while. John and Devon said Cameron would really feel his labors had been in vain if they gave in to this pressure. Joy said the only way they could show support was to continue on until Cam was back with them. Inside, she wondered just how long that would be.

Mrs. Thompson had secured a number of the special, blue books like Gabe had presented to her. She had bought them for the group out of some of the more than expected payment she'd received from Gabe for her car. Most of the Commune's families studied this book daily and reviewed with their friends on Sunday gatherings. It was sure altering their way of thinking. Their newly acquired positive attitudes were really manifesting in prosperity. At least, until this new challenge arose with Cameron's false charges.

Organized religion was fearful of the new political system and also of the new age thinkers. They felt it their duty to wage spiritual war on both. In fact, it was hinted that a fundamental Christian group had directed the Government's attention to Cameron. What they were not aware of was that new age spirituality was just another channel of the same God teachings but not so fear-controlled.

Mrs. Thompson reminded the group they must not harbor ill feelings towards the religious activists or the fear-controlled politicians. She read where "God does not forgive because He has never condemned. And there must be condemnation before forgiveness is necessary. Forgiveness is the great need of this world, but that is because it is a world of illusions. Those who forgive are thus releasing themselves from illusions, while those who withhold forgiveness are binding themselves to them." *(A Course In Miracles)*

It was three in the morning when Dana was awakened by a knock on her door. "Grandma, I think it's time for you to play doctor," Joy announced. Dana's legs suddenly felt lifeless and would not cooperate with her attempt to rise out of her bed. "You awake, Grandmother?" Joy's voice sounded a little more urgent this time.

"Doc" Dana had been well programmed for this moment and was proceeding like a pro. Joy Dean was certainly doing her part by breathing and pushing in a controlled rhythm. Joy was a lot more confident of Dana's performance than her own. Oh, how she wished Cam was here to hold her hand and send her love energy.

Derek had heard the commotion, jumped out of bed, dressed, and rushed over to get Cameron's parents. Amy came fussing in so excitedly that Dana tactfully busied her with heating water and making coffee to get her out of her delivery room. Then it happened—the head of their firstborn slid out into the world, followed by a perfect, little male body. They had done it! Baby Townsend had arrived! Then, before the family had time to be introduced to the newcomer, Joy Dean went into labor again. Male child number two followed his brother into this world only fifteen minutes later.

The family was elated, except for the vacancy felt for the missing father. Joy Dean had said that her and Cam had already decided on the name John if it was a boy. They had chosen that name to honor Cam's father and the disciple—John's name stood for love.

Grandpa John was bursting with pride of the acknowledgement given to him. He recalled what Gabe had told him about his seeing his grandchildren play on this farm...and wept with joy. If only he could have shared this moment of bliss with his son, his joy would have been complete. Again he wept.

Joy Dean decided to call the other baby James. The disciple James was known for wisdom. She felt love and wisdom was a combination the present world needed.

The Tele-Com alerted the family a communication was incoming. It was Cam. He looked thinner, but very good to his family standing around the communication center. He was being released with a full pardon, as they could not find any grounds solid enough to convict him. He would be flying into the airport in Orlando tomorrow and take the monorail home. This time he assured Joy he would be home for supper!

Joy was elated! Dana and Joy each held up one of the twins for Cam to see. He had not even been informed of their births and then to see double blessings turned him speechless—he just grinned and a few tears found their way down his cheek as he waved a goodbye. Tomorrow he would be able to hold his baby sons, now five months old.

Derek had received his Master's and was feeling quite pleased with this achievement. Yet, he again was entertaining a restless spirit and was anxious to begin creating his dream. Dana watched the telltale signs and knew soon she would have to say goodbye. Her heart also told her it would not be forever.

Dana's days were busy again helping with the twins. It reminded her of the days when Derek and Joy Dean were so young and she became their caretaker. The twins were sure robust, muscular, energetic little guys. Joy had been exquisite like her mother, and Derek like a Grecian Adonis. The twins were more like their Grandpa John. James was the larger of the fraternal twins and the instigator of their adventures. John had more of Joy's finer features and showed a more passive, gentler nature.

Joy Dean was once more very active in caring for the sick and sharing her healing abilities. Cameron was once more involved in community affairs, both theirs and new ones appearing on the scene. Joy still worried about the repercussions from the government over Cam's endeavors, but knew he would do what he had to do anyway, so she tried not to dwell on the negatives. John and Devon had all they could do to attend to the farm—they were not as young and energetic as their yesterdays. Amy and Dana shared a lot of the chores, food preserving, and babysitting duties. They also shared hopes, dreams, and even fears. They had become the closest of friends. Derek tried to contribute to the wellbeing of the farm, but it was an effort that was not backed by heart interest.

What a surprise to all when the Tele-Com alerted the family of an incoming message and they viewed their old friend, Gabe, on the screen. He chatted with the family, congratulated Cam and Joy over their double blessing, filled them in on his comings and goings, and asked to speak to Derek. Derek was listening intently as Gabe addressed him. "Want to pursue a dream?" Gabe then informed him how he had sold his trucks on the mainland for enough credits to become a partner in an air-freight service. It was out of Orlando and extended to Denver with mid-stop at Nashville. He was making a run to Denver tomorrow, and had heard they were in need of building engineers there. "Would Derek be interested?" Gabe questioned his friend. One look at Derek's face answered that question. "Yes, yes, yes!" shouted Derek. Gabe chuckled, "I guess that means you would like to go." Gabe told him to be at the Orlando Airport Friday at 8 a.m. sharp. Gabe told the rest of the family goodbye and his image left the screen.

Friday morning before sunrise, Devon, Dana and Derek loaded into the car along with a heavy trunk of Derek's belongings. Derek gazed back at the farm barely visible in the predawn light as they drove down the long drive to the highway. He wondered if he would ever do any living there again or if this was a chapter of his life closing. He would miss his family and friends very much, but the call of his dream was so strong he had to answer it. He had felt that "tap" on his shoulder and couldn't ignore it.

Gabe was waiting at Aircraft Hanger number nine as he had informed his friends. He sure looked healthy and well-minded. Devon was so glad to see him again, and they gave each other a big bear hug. He visited with them for a brief time and then apologized that it could not be longer. "Have a schedule to keep. Let's load up, Derek."

Dana felt her heart sink as "her boy" gave her a hug and assured his grandmother that this was but a temporary separation. "I'm going to create a dream for us both, Grandma. You will see it as the finished product. I promise!" The two boarded, engines roared, wheels taxied the big freighter down the runway...and lift off. Devon and Dana watched as the sky miniaturized the craft into nothingness. The ride back to the farm was long and silent, each passenger trying to fill that vacant spot in their heart with memories and expectations.

13

Caught In the Balance

IT HAD BEEN ALMOST a year since Derek had left the farm. They had heard from him two or three times on the Tele-Com. He had looked so content and at peace with his life. The last time he called, he had introduced the family to Taylor. She was a design architect also, and worked at the same firm as Derek. They had become best of friends, and were considering seeing if their relationship was ready to go beyond friendship to a more lasting commitment. They had become roommates, and the arrangement seemed to be quite compatible to both.

The family liked her appearance, and they trusted Derek's judgment. Besides, she seemed to be very supportive of Derek; they appeared good for each other. So, the family voted to accept her into the clan. They told Taylor they were looking forward to meeting her in person, and told Derek how much he was missed on the farm. They wished them well and urged them to keep in touch.

Derek had told them of the possibility of Taylor and him being sent by the firm to this undeveloped area in the far northeast corner of Colorado. They were to check out the site as a possible location for a new kind of city to be built there. It would be a model of futuristic possibilities. If they were chosen, Derek and Taylor would try for a quick visit to the farm before relocating. Everyone was delighted over this great news and anticipated hearing further on this development.

In general, World citizens were becoming more free-thinking and not so dependent upon their government for their needs. They were not even as comfortable with the previously praised credit system. They were getting suspicious that the "chip" was controlling a lot more of their life than they were informed of. What secret manipulations were affecting their lifestyles and mental faculties, they wondered.

The Council met at Geneva to access this increasing distrust and rebelliousness against authority. It was becoming contagious and needed to be attended to now!

Epsolum Petra was well aware of this growing self-minded attitude pervading the population. He had created a much safer world with the decrease in crime and drug abuse, which perhaps had contributed to the people's rising confidence. Then, a higher force was using Mother Nature's influence to awaken a passive planet. People were either growing strong and independent, or panicky and non-functioning. Petra could take care of the "disabled" as the chip would activate an elimination body-process to begin. It was those emerging "Davids" daring to take on government "Goliaths" that was unsettling to him. He knew to that control people, you must control their mind. He thought of himself as a caring father dealing with unruly children. He had to find a way to get them back under his patriarchal wings. He also could not accept losing any of his newfound power.

Epsolum knew the criminal affluence in society was not controllable, but that a drug-dependent individual could be dominated easily as they had already enslaved themselves to the addiction.

Once again the Council was called, but not fully taken into confidence by "Father." Petra explained the advantages of creating "pleasure houses" to relieve present day societal tensions. People would have a place to go to relax and escape the fears and pressures of present times. This would be a mind altering psychedelic atmosphere. It would have hypnotic music piped in, along with an intoxicating aroma that when breathed in created a feeling of ecstasy. What the Council was not informed of was the addictive power of this gaseous drug and the gradual personality alterations it evoked upon the unsuspecting public. It made them into docile, passive and controllable beings.

And so, society was introduced to an exciting new media of "unwinding" and pleasure. Careful sexual practices were abandoned in this state of euphoria, and the previous decline in AIDS shot upwards quickly.

This was being thoroughly discussed at the Sunday gathering at the Community Center. Mainly, the new pleasure houses were being introduced into the larger cities and did not as yet really affect the more rural sections like Devon's neighborhood.

Just as interesting, and maybe more because of its more positive countenance, was talk of the new President.

He had only been in for not quite a year, but was already either endearing himself or being ostracized by his fellow Americans. The fundamental religious denominations had backed him as a "born again" leader. Now, there was a split in their support as some thought he had sold out to a new age way of thinking. Regardless of how his religious beliefs were perceived, he was seen as a high-minded man. He had been elected on a non-party affiliation ticket, which was a first for the country. He believed party values had only served to separate the country, and this was a time for unity. He was a good man, and was working to bring security to the land. He was working with scientists and others to map out geographical areas safe from nature's disasters. He was alerting the people not only in the states, but other nations' leaders of dangerous and safe places. He seemed to have special insight into future possibilities. He was sponsoring projects in those sections deemed safe so people could move there and find employment.

Derek had the pleasure of meeting the President when a number of invited designers and scientists were called to meet with him to discuss the possibility of implementing these projects. One of the areas fingered for materialization was a futuristic model city in Colorado.

The President's wife, and helpmate, was urging the American people to promote healthy lifestyles. A strong people was needed to help this country survive. This was the outer facade of Epsolum's program, but it stopped at a healthy body—not mind.

Joy Dean heartily endorsed the First Lady's program because she knew a healthy body was a positive force for good. She was becoming more of an herbalist and "mind-over-matter" physician than the old pill and cut days. She rarely used prescription drugs. She was also accepting the gift of healing the Universe had bestowed upon her. She had witnessed many times how the touch of her hands on ailing parts of a body seemed to alleviate the discomfort or eliminate the problem totally. She also remembered how years ago, when Derek and she were young, Grandma Dana would have them take natural vitamins and anti-toxin fortifiers. They were never sick like the other neighborhood children, and bounced back quicker when they did catch something. Perhaps keeping healthy also helped them to face life's challenges with a more positive attitude—well body, well mind. She knew that more and more people were turning away from professional medical help, listening to their own body talk to them, rejecting prescription medicines, and utilizing natures' healing resources. It was almost as if the earth and its inhabitants were uniting to assist each other in a healing.

The farm was in need of a pick-me-up shot in the arm. Derek would be the one to deliver it via the Tele-Com. Once again, Dana was viewing "her boy" on the screen. He looked good, but more mature. He told Dana to bake some good homemade bread. He would be home to enjoy it before it was cool enough to slice.

Taylor and he had been commissioned to start drafting the blueprints of the President's proposed "new city!" They would relocate in the designated building area in two weeks. They were planning to visit Taylor's family at Little Rock, Arkansas, and then spend a few days on the farm. They would be there next Thursday and leave out the following Monday. He would be able to see all of his friends at the Sunday meeting.

The farm came alive with preparation activities. Everyone was so excited about Derek's brief homecoming. Dana could hardly wait; it had been so long since she had been able to fuss over her grandson. The twins were caught up in the excitement of "Unkie Dek's" visit although they really didn't remember him.

Word went out to the neighbors and all began planning a festive Sunday. It had been a long time since the Commune had a reason to celebrate, and they planned to make this a gala affair. They even collected a couple of antique electric ice cream makers to provide the touch to the homemade goodies the ladies were al busy baking. Yes, Sunday would be a day to remember!

14
The Dream

THURSDAY MORNING EARLY found Cameron and Dana on their way to Orlando Airport to pick up Derek and Taylor. Joy knew how much this reunion meant to her grandmother, and convinced her to ride with Cam. She would stay with Devon and the twins.

"There they are, I see them!" Dana was shouting and waving. Derek's strong arms were entwining her small waist, and he was lifting and twirling her around like she was a small child. Finally, he gently brought her down for a landing and guided her over to Taylor.

Dana and Taylor's eyes met and in that instant they knew they had a bond...their love for Derek. There was another connection taking place. They both knew they had important roles in influencing Derek to accomplish what he knew he was on earth to do. "Thank you for coming. You are as beautiful in person as on the screen. I'm so glad you are now a part of Derek's life. I think he has always been waiting for you." Dana hugged Taylor and then turned back to drink in the sight of her grandson again. Cam and Derek were shaking hands and slapping each other playfully on the back in greeting. They were an exuberant bunch as the miles disappeared, making the long awaited homecoming closer and closer.

Devon was waiting on the porch and bounded down the steps to give Derek the old bear hug greeting. Joy Dean was close behind with a couple of curious two-year-olds peeking around their mother's skirt. John and Amy waited until later to make an appearance to give the family a little personal time.

Everyone was so excited that the evening meal was hardly touched. They then did their evening ritual of journeying out to the yard chairs. John and Amy joined them, and they all talked 'til past midnight. The farm then gave way to the quiet of the night and its occupants succumbed to a peaceful sleep.

Derek had a visitation some time before dawn. Whether it was a dream, a vision, or an out-of-body experience was not clear, but the details were permanently etched into his memory.

The next morning, Derek was still mulling over the happening. Even though he was thrilled to be back on the farm with his family again, he was noticeably quiet.

Dana sensed there was something distracting her grandson's mental attention away from the activities going on around the breakfast table. Something he was not ready to share with the group. She suggested they walk to the pond for a few moments of selfish time. He seemed eager to oblige, and they slipped out the door unnoticed. The twins were busy entertaining Taylor with their antics. Joy Dean was just finishing clearing the table, and Cam and Devon were deep in discussion about Sunday's activities.

Derek took his grandmother by the arm as they headed down that old familiar path he had taken so many times with his fishing pole. "Are you happy?" Dana inquired. "Very, Grandmother. I feel really alive for the first time. I'm not just sure what is ahead for me, but I know it has already begun. Then, it feels so right with Taylor. I can't explain the feeling. It is like I've always known she was out there waiting for me. I have always felt only half alive, and she makes me feel complete and whole." "I know," Dana commented, "together you can work miracles." "You could make it really perfect by coming back with us." Derek looked at his grandmother with the "please" look that always turned her to putty. She would so love to do that but right now was not the time. She didn't donate a lot of physical energy anymore to the running of the farm, but she was their "safety net" and stabilizing influence. She couldn't abandon them now. "Not right yet, my boy, maybe later," she reasoned. "Okay, but there will be a right time, and I will send for you," Derek said in a no further discussion tone.

Now, there is something else on your mind. Come sit here by me and let's talk." Dana motioned for Derek to sit on the bank by her.

"It is this dream or something weird that happened this morning. I'm not sure just what took place, but it was as real as us sitting here. Yes, I need to tell someone, and I'm really glad it is you." With that, Derek bean a most unusual tale:

"It seemed like I was awakened by a presence in the room. I thought at first it might be one of the family, but there was no one visible—just light illuminating the corner of the room and the feeling of an unknown presence or more than one. No verbal conversation, and yet, I found myself communicating with it with no difficulty. It was telling me to come with them, to trust, and I would see things not yet seen."

"I wasn't sure where we were to go or how, it didn't even seem important to ask. I was in bed with Taylor beside me. I even knew we were in my old room on the farm, and then suddenly, I was soaring through a tranquil, dark space. It was neither frightening nor exciting, it just was. I don't know how long, time did not seem to exist as we know it."

"My next awareness was in this chamber that was so intensely illuminated it should have been blinding me, yet I didn't even squint; and the clarity of images was indescribable."

"Our President was sitting across from this light being. There was a scroll or parchment on a crystal, glass-like table between them. The President seemed to be consulting with the being, and then they turned to face me. They motioned for me to join. Again, there was no physical gestures or verbalization, I just knew what they wanted."

"The President was explaining how he was being shown places on Earth that would survive coming disaster, and how best to utilize these areas to benefit the survival and restoration of mankind and his planet."

"They were explaining my role in this coming era. I was to be the architect that would build the "city of hope"—it would be the first born of the Golden Age. It would be called "Providence." It was also shown to me that this city had been mentally designed years before by another earth dreamer. The blueprint had been saved in the ethereal space until time for the "chosen" to receive it. The dreamer would then pass on this to the heir...I was that one."

"I was again in this dark space, only this time the darkness was transformed into a sea of lights. There, below me, was the most fantastic city of my wildest dreams. I soared and weaved, I felt and touched, I explored the heights and depths, and finally I personally internalized every square inch of this city. It was photographed in my never-to-be-forgotten mind. I knew this was truly my city, my dream!"

Then, without effort, I was opening my eyes and gazing around the almost distinguishable features of the bedroom that was lit slightly by the first rays of this day."

"I can't even begin to describe what I'm feeling, but I want to experience it again. I think I will. I also think that just maybe, I visited my future last night!"

What could Dana say to that tale except to tell Derek to hold tight to that experience, for it would provide him the energy and courage to push that door of tomorrow open.

Joy Dean and Taylor were heading down the path to the pond. Derek and Dana sealed their secret with a hug, and then he jaunted off to meet Taylor and show her around the farm. The next couple of days, time stood still on the farm, and the world outside it did not exist. Dana's family became whole and happy again...at least for a while.

Sunday was the icing on the cake. The celebration lasted well past sunset. Derek somehow knew he would never watch another Florida sunset. He also knew miles would never separate him from his family and friends. Love knows not distance.

Dana told them goodbye at the farm this time. She could not trust her emotions for another airport farewell. She would stay with the twins and allow Joy Dean and Cameron to make this trip.

Dana hugged Taylor and gave her special blessings for a happy life. She then hugged "her boy," and couldn't quite prevent a couple tears from sliding down her now gracefully aging cheeks. "Grandma, the next tears I see on that face will be tears of joy when you come to live with me. Don't forget, I'll be sending for you!" With that, they waved to the family, loaded into the car that would take Derek away from the farm for the last time.

15

The Day Time Blinked

EARTH-SPACE 1 was about to undergo a shift change. It was time for Shift Two to begin. Earth's day and night time intervals were not on similar daylight and dark schedules because of the orbit path of the space station. Three shifts were mandated to give equal time for work, play and rest. This also provided an alert, on-task crew at all times.

The space station had been a reality for almost a decade. Earth-Space 2 was in the process of being completed on the far side of the moon. There was talk of the possibility of construction soon to begin an Earth 3 close to the planet Mars.

Earth 1 has an increasing population of some 700-800 inhabitants. It was a varied population consisting of scientists, astronauts, medical and mechanical technicians, crew, and even some family members, including children.

They had five shuttle docking ramps, and always kept two ready for liftoffs. They frequently had visiting dignitaries and space administrators make check-up arrivals. The incoming shuttle would be docked for refueling and maintenance checks while a prepared shuttle would make the return trip to the planet.

The station had diligently been studying the Phatron Belt running midway around Earth. It acted as an electronic magnetic shield. In the past eight months, there had been sun flares of such magnitude that immense streams of damaging rays were reaching earth's surface. Its effects could not be ignored, although scientists witnessed both a positive and negative reaction occurring. It appeared to be having a purification action on the problem of air pollution. But, it also was causing a melting of glaciers and icebergs, which was drastically affecting ocean levels and currents, and eventually weather deviations. Flooding and famines were occurring in previously fertile, food bearing areas. The problem of skin cancers was increasing.

There were even a number of unexplainable happenings of people incinerating by an apparent internal combustion. It was wondered if the solar flares were factors to be considered.

The most notable job Earth-Space 1 would be remembered for would be the recording and witnessing of the phenomenal moment of the shifting of Earth's magnetic poles. It was so instantaneous and unexpected that had it not been recorded by the electronic eyes on the space station. Earth may have not understood the total impact of the occurrence for years.

Edgar Cayce and many others spoke of a pole shift that was to take place near the end of the century, and of radical changes in seasons. For years, the weather had been very erratic and unpredictable. Since Earth was over a decade into the 21st century, old predictions were all but forgotten.

There had been numerous signs that a possible planetary alteration could be imminent, but scientists and government leaders weren't proclaiming their concerns to the public since they had enough to exist sanely with already.

Wind currents had made noticeable shifts in patterns, the seas had risen in some areas and sunk in others in proportion to the adjoining land, and some areas had even broken up, causing cave-ins and other small calamities.

During this period of Earth's shaking and rocking, earthquake and volcano activity started deep in the ocean floor around the Bahama Islands. This was affecting the coastal areas of Florida from around Melbourne to the south of

Miami with extreme high tides and tidal waves, destroying beaches and coastal properties. When the activity finally stopped, Florida's landscape had been drastically changed. Below sea level, mountain ranges now had risen to the surface. The Great Bahama Bank had emerged upwards to visible heights. The Bahama Islands were now connected to Florida's east coast. New inland rivers and lakes were formed. Lake Okeechobee had expanded its banks south to Homestead with huge fingers of waterways past Ft. Myers to the Gulf. Sanibel Island was all but annihilated.

This was considered a devastating catastrophe at the time, but was most likely Florida's salvation from the Atlantic's "big sloshing" that devoured other areas during its present shifting around. It had created new beaches and inlets on the seaside of the Bahamas and northern Florida coasts, but inland was fairly protected.

According to the space station, all action on Earth took place in an instant—in a blink of time. Most of the space station dwellers were not even a witness until they watched the reruns and tried to figure out what had just taken place on their Mother planet.

When the planet decided to realign its magnetic pole position, it dipped the North Pole out into the Pacific Ocean, freezing the water to great depths immediately. It shifted the South Pole to the lower portion of South America and instantly preserved all life forms in a frozen state of arctic cold.

This was not Earth's first realignment. As early as 50,000 B.C. and later, the planet had given in to the imbalances and corrected itself. This not only occurred on Earth, but other planetary systems. Yet, to the survivors on Earth and the spectators in space, this was the only one that mattered.

Earth locked in to its new position and completed its facial reconstruction, along with a needed purification of its gases and liquids. The tip of South American was now the new Antarctic, and where the Pacific previously flowed was now the Glaciers of the new North Pole. The North Pole was now positioned in the Aleutian Trench about 150-200 miles south of the Aleutian Islands.

The land connecting North and South American had given way to the Gulf waters and now rested below sea level. Many European lowlands had succumbed to the ocean's sloshing across its land. Coastal areas throughout the world were affected to greater or lesser degrees.

Florida had changed its latitude and longitude settings, and now resided in a new position of a few degrees above the equator. It was, even now, feeling the atmospheric changes of heat and moisture. These climate changes were to affect the quick foliage growth of the new landmass that was now part of Florida and the Bahamas.

It was theorized that Earth had become lopsided from buildup of snow and ice at poles, and from the oceans cutting away and rearranging the landmasses. Oil and water removal from Earth had heightened the unbalancing factor. Then, some pull from outer space was suspected as certain planets had lined up to produce a heavy pull.

The ozone layer and sunlight was believed to contribute to the warming trend just preceding the earth's shift. It caused polar ice caps to melt and sea levels to be drastically affected.

The people on Earth who survived, and there was a large number, had a massive undertaking during the reconstruction period. Many who did not safely ride out the shift were instantly frozen; or, along coastal areas, swept out to sea, posing no health problems for the survivors. There was a need for mass burials for victims of falling buildings and such. There was little time for mourning, as the survivors needed all their attention directed towards sustaining their own self and family's wellbeing.

Rubbish was cleared very quickly and people began to be their brother's keeper. Electricity still existed in some scattered areas. Nuclear wastes gave some concern, but were quickly resolved. Enlightenment seemed to flow to this new race, and they found ways to grow crops more speedily, and erect dwellings that required little time or energy.

It was ushering in a new time of love and understanding, of consideration and compassion, and of joyous awakening to the reality that we are all one.

It was a time of discovering again the joy of making things by hand, and cooperating with neighbors and friends. As a more spiritual race began to unfold, the universe seemed to respond and the beginnings of a "golden age" was birthed. It ushered in the finest period that Earth had known since the early beginnings when beings were in communication with the Creative Force.

The Christ spirit began to manifest its presence, and as it joined mankind's awareness, people's eyes opened to the reality that it is all one world in different vibratory levels. Minds became open to their own inner vibrations. No more was the need for sects, divisions, and so-called religious wars. Weapons no longer needed were recast into plows.

16
Exit the Dark

IT HAD BEEN A FEW DAYS since Dana had made the walk down to the pond. It was harder for her to get around these days. Devon had built a bench for his mother on the bank of the pond. It was difficult for Dana to master getting down to ground level, and even harder to get up.

She loved to sit here and reminisce how it used to be on the farm before "the shift" and the bad winds. It was harder to adapt to changes than a few years ago, she thought.

It had been over four years since Derek and she had sat here on the bank of the pond and shared their dreams. She wondered if "her boy" ever had a chance to begin his city. Really, what she most wanted to know, but wouldn't let her mind think on, was if Taylor and he had survived "the shift." They had received no word about them. She also wondered what Derek would think of the farm if he could visit it now.

Even the vegetation around the pond had changed. The sandy bank, lily pads, and cattails, plus the orchard and garden, were all replaced or overgrown with ferns, palms and viney plants.

She tried real hard to visualize the farm of her earlier and happier years, but even when she closed her eyes, the mental pictures would fade quicker than she could conjure them up. It seemed useless to try to dwell in those days. Perhaps her attentions needed to be on today.

Had it really only been three years ago when everything changed so quickly? she wondered. "Yes. In fact, it was the day of my 70th birthday celebration," Dana verbalized to the silent pond. Dana remembered that Joy Dean had invited several of the neighbors with whom they were on more intimate terms over for a chicken fry and some watermelon. She reminisced how they had set up several tables outside, and they were laden with food and desserts the neighbors and Joy had prepared. Some of the older neighborhood children were playing yard games with the twins. The men were playing horseshoes. Dana...well, she remembered sitting in the big yard chair like a Queen Bee observing her royal beehive drones. How perfect this day would have been, she remembered thinking, if only Taylor and Derek would drive up!

Derek had called her that morning on the Tele-Com to wish her happy birthday and to remind her of his promise to send for her. He had explained how they were running into a lot of legal setbacks and delays in receiving promised funding. He was sure they would be breaking ground real soon, though, and still sounded so enthused. That was the last conversation she had had with her grandson. She wondered if he ever got started building that special city.

Dana mentally meandered back to when she first moved out to the farm. How different it looked now. It was the winds —the horrible, horrendous winds. They were lucky that any of them survived those dark hours.

There she was, one moment watching her family and friends, listening to the laughter and squeals of the children, the clank-clank of the horseshoes contacting the metal posts, and the soft chatter of the ladies setting the table. Suddenly, the ground beneath their feet went into what felt like a giant hiccup! What was happening was on all their minds, but before they had a chance to gather their senses, a deadening roar began. "Tornado!" someone yelled, and instinctively all grabbed the kids and headed for the root cellar. They huddled together in the small area and listened for hours to what sounded like the lost and damned of the ages shrieking and wailing. It was the most frightening sound Dana ever remembered hearing and one she would never forget.

Even now she could almost feel the fear of the group, feel the warmness of the air, hear the cries of the frightened children, and recall the total blackness of the cellar. The adults were praying and pleading to an unseen Protector to please save this little group from the raging elements beyond the cellar door. They knew an angel of mercy was holding the door from flying off from the force of the wind. After hours and hours of fearful anticipation, it was quiet. Too quiet. The men pushed up the door and tried to look out, but it was too dark to survey the storm's damage. They had decided it best to wait in the cellar for dawn, but with the door opened for air. They all remarked how hot and humid the night air felt, which was unusual for this time of year. The women settled the children on to their laps on the floor of the cellar, and the men sat guard on the steps.

As the first glimmer of dawn broke, the group had emerged, not knowing what sight would greet them. There was devastation everywhere. It was impossible to absorb all at once. Devon checked the house first and found it partially standing.

Most of the roof was gone, and part of the back porch and kitchen collapsed or had blown away.

The barn was not much more than a foundation. It wasn't until later that they discovered the bodies of the horses and calves that had been housed in the barn. The cows had not been brought in for milking yet, so if they hadn't been killed by flying debris, they had wandered away to other areas. They did find about ten that were injured but alive. The hen house and chickens did not fare as well, nothing salvageable on either counts.

Down by the pond was where Amy and John's home used to exist. Now, there was a partial wall of a bathroom, a broken bathtub, and some twisted plumbing pipes. That was all.

Trees throughout the orchard and yard were uprooted or snapped in two. Several cars were squashed by big limbs of fallen trees or tossed and laid crumpled out in the field.

The strangest part of the whole disaster inventory was the temperature. It had been a pleasant, somewhat breezy fall day before the storm. Upon leaving the cellar and even before the sun was very high in the sky, the air was extremely most and very warm. It stayed warm, even after the rains. Sometimes it would rain for days.

They had searched the house and yard for anything that could help them survive for a few days. They all bunked in what was left of Devon's house, which were several bedrooms and a partial living room. They used the fireplace to cook in when the weather was bad, and a makeshift grill for outside.

A couple of days after the storm, the men pieced together a workable vehicle and ventured out to check the state of their neighbors' homes. The neighbors visiting were especially anxious to go see how their places had survived, if they had.

They were not real successful finding much of anything, but collected a few belongings to come back for. A few chickens were captured, and even a few head of cattle. They even found a truck that had been protected by a big tree that had held it down without damaging the motor; just damaged the looks of it. They loaded all they could and Cam followed the others back in the truck.

The men also found a small number of the community members alive, but frightened and bewildered. They invited them to join the others at the farm or help them to join more fortunate neighbors to start their own little groups. Sadly, there were also a small number of friends that had not been so lucky. They did their best to give them a respectful burial, but had not the energy or time to give in to grief.

Over the next year, the farm had gathered six more families besides Devon and John's. Their extended family had taken over the old home. They had added four more bedrooms plus rebuilding the damaged but still standing four rooms. John and Amy, Joy and Cam, Devon, Dana, the twins, and even baby Charity each had their own private space. They had a spare room for unexpected guests, and one that hopefully some day Derek and Taylor could use. They had enlarged and restored the big sitting room, and added a big, new fireplace. It was more for looks; what with this new climate, it probably would never be needed. The kitchen was where most of the family's daylight hours would take place, and so they made it as huge and inviting as possible. One long harvest table became the conversation arena. A lot of discouragements were shared there, along with the moments of frivolity. They used this area as their educational center, their game table, their office, and their church. It was still too difficult to gather at the Commune Center anymore; besides, three families had made it into living quarters. So the table often even served as the Center for their own little group on the farm.

It was not as easy as before to travel any distance. So pleasure driving was not an option—only for necessities. Solar cards were becoming available from the mainland, but most people couldn't afford them. At the farm, they had purchased two to be used as needed by all the families. The also had one community truck which was motorized by nuclear batteries. Since there were six families living on the farm, besides John and Devon's car, usage was limited.

Four families had used the old barn foundation and built a two story, four family dwelling. A duplex was built on the area where the chicken house once stood. It really looked like a commune now. They had all worked together and built three small barns and a grain storage bin.

The whole neighborhood shared livestock and feed, as the little groups needed them. No one ever hoarded food or possessions anymore. Surpluses were always divided, and shortages supplied when possible. Gardens produced profusely with the year round growing seasons. The root cellar was too moist to keep produce, so they either canned, dried or shared.

Dana had performed her last midwife duty when Joy Dean had Charity. Joy Dean was back on staff now as "Doc." She no longer used any medication other than natural herbs or nature provided remedies. Her gift of healing energy that flowed through her hands had alleviated many physical ailments without the need for medicinal attending.

Cameron was becoming the prominent agricultural advisor throughout the Florida Island, even the new Bahama section. The lush Bahama valleys nestled on each side of the mountains were providing much of the tropical fruits and vegetables for Florida's consumption, and for bartering for supplies on the mainland. Cameron was provided a vehicle to get around in, free usage of the reconstructed monorails, and even air transportation if needed. Joy hated him being gone so much but couldn't travel with him because she was needed at home.

Bartering was still the most effective means of exchanging goods and services throughout the world. The IDI chip was still recognized as a monetary exchange system, but had been downgraded immensely. It seemed that shortly after the "shift," a group of zealots led by a disgruntled Council member in Switzerland had decided "Father" Petra was trying to play God and needed dethroning. The plan was to call an emergency meeting to discuss the communication problems that had occurred from the power outages throughout the land, shutting down so many relay computers.

The zealots were to be hired to serve refreshments and attend to the needs of the Council. The meeting lasted for close to 14 hours, and all were exhausted. The Council member who had originated the plan asked Petra to stay for a private information session. They had settled back into a private conversation area and were indulging in a glass of premium wine served by one of the plotters. Petra's glass contained an undetectable analgesic.

Petra never even sensed what had transpired. After he served as a hand identification means to gain entry into "Mother's Chamber," his body was air transported and disposed of somewhere over the new Arctic's frozen surface. All that the world knew at the time was that Petra had deprogrammed his brainchild. Its only function was to act as a credit accountant for credit deposits, withdrawals and transfers. It no longer controlled life spans, body functions, or held personal information to be used on its slaves. It was years later, during a state of intoxication, one of the zealots boasted of his part in the dethroning plan.

The cities, especially ones with towering buildings, suffered the most destruction from the shift and the post-shift winds. Slowly, rebuilding was taking place, and both nuclear and solar power was returning life to the cities and rural areas. Mass transit systems were replacing individual transport vehicles.

Air passenger and freights were becoming the connecting roadways to the mainland and to other countries. Florida was no longer feeling totally isolated.

Gigantic nuclear submarines were being utilized to test possibilities of ocean bottom labs or stations being erected. Already large amounts of food and energy resources were being derived from the oceans. Water and wind currents were being harnessed for energy sources very successfully. The people of Earth were a lot more environmentally conscious and aware of nature's value to their very existence. There was now a compatible partnership between mankind and his planet. They did not wish to anger or upset "Mother Nature's" sense of balance every again!

Government was not in a ruling capacity as much as a caretaker's role. Communities, cities, and districts pretty much determined their own needs and found ways to meet them. The President was more a Counselor to these areas and a representative to leaders of other countries. The same president that had held office just before the shift was reelected. He had earned his people's trust.

Communication was still slow to become as available as pre-shift days. Tele-Com had become useless in many areas, especially the rural ones. Most of the relay towers had been destroyed by the big wind. Technology was installing satellite-to-satellite voice transmitters. Individuals, for the most part, could not afford the personal satellite receivers, and so would use community owned ones. The farm had not yet been able to invest in one, nor their neighbors.

Dana missed the Tele-Com the most. She had no way of seeing or talking to "her boy." Somehow, though, from deep inside her heart, she just knew that someday Derek would keep his promise. He would find a way to get in touch. He would send for her! She had to believe that. It was the motivation that made her open her eyes to each new tomorrow.

Dana felt the oppressive noonday heat and decided it was time to leave her seat by the pond and get back to the coolness of the solar cooled house. Dana thought to herself, as she slowly meandered back to the farmhouse, "I miss you Derek. I am ready now to leave the farm and join you. I pray you are receiving these thoughts wherever you are."

17

Welcome To Providence

JOY DEAN FIXED SOME peppermint tea for the Johnson's eight-year-old daughter. Seems like she had eaten some not ripe avocados and had a tummy ache. The thought that since the shift, her services were no longer needed for serious illnesses. It was almost as if the winds had blown the germs and viruses into outer space. Perhaps Earth had gone through a purification. She hadn't heard of a case of AIDS in years, and colds or flu symptoms were almost unheard of.

Another thing Joy had noticed of late was people seemed to be much more perceptive and relied on their intuition more than their once rigid logical reasoning. People seemed to be more in tune with each other, too, and often, without speaking a word, they would sense what the other was thinking or feeling.

Right now, Joy Dean was sensing that Cam was heading for the farm, although he wasn't due for another three days. She also felt an aura of excitement surrounding him, but couldn't perceive the cause.

She took the tea over to the Johnson's, checked their daughter Beth, chatted for a few minutes, and excused herself. She was anxious to get back to the house, though there was nothing pressing for her to do there.

Dana was snapping green beans for supper and looked up at Joy Dean. Joy had been looking out the window towards the drive at least a dozen times. "What is wrong with you, child?" Dana inquired, with a touch of curiosity in her voice. "You weren't this restless when you waited for your Dad to get dressed for your wedding." "Grandma, I wish I knew, but I will real soon. We both will...I just feel it!" Well, thought Dana, that's as much clarity on the matter she would get for now, so...

Whatever was making Joy Dean anxious was now pulling up to the front of the house and shutting two car doors. This action caused the reaction of the front door to be swung open and an excited woman to run out onto the porch. "Cam! I knew you were coming home this evening!" Joy shouted a greeting to her husband. Then, startled at recognizing the other passenger, Joy raised her voice again. "Gabe! Is that really you?" this caught Dana's attention and she nearly dumped the bowl of beans onto the floor in her haste to verify what she heard.

There he stood in the doorway, just a-grinning. Gabe felt like he was returning home, but is surely didn't look like the home he remembered. Dana couldn't believe her eyes, it was truly Gabe. She tried to look beyond him to the still open door—dared she hope? Was Derek about to walk through the door next? Gabe caught her inquisitive expression and knew who she was really looking for.

Joy Dean and Cameron came in and shut the door. Dana knew that was the answer to her momentary expectation. After greetings, Gabe directed his first conversation to Dana. He said it had been a couple of years since he had seen Derek. It was at the Denver air fright terminal, and Derek was there to check on some special building materials. He had taken the time to look up Gabe, and spent a few quick hours visiting with him. Derek was beginning to oversee some model city project up in the northwest section of Colorado. Taylor was working with him, but didn't do much traveling then, as she was pregnant.

Dana was drinking in all of this information, and was overjoyed to hear Derek was okay. He had survived the shift—he was evidently doing what he was destined to do—and he was going to make Dana a great-grandmother again!

John, Amy, Devon and the rest of the family kept Gabe talking until almost dawn. They had so many questions to ask and experiences to share—sleep would have been impossible.

Cameron explained how surprised he was when he had gone to the airfreight terminal to pick up some hybrid seed he had requested from the mainland, to find out who had flown them in. Gabe had a two-day layover, and Cam talked him into a quick visit to the farm. He would take him back tomorrow afternoon.

Gabe shared the sad news that his mother had lost her life in the post-shift windstorm. He was in Denver at the time and felt real remorse for not being here with her. "You told us that our lives are ordered and that there is nothing by chance," John reminded him. "Thank you, my friend. That's true," Gabe responded.

Gabe couldn't believe all the changes that had taken place on the farm. He also saw how his friend Dana had aged. He realized how much she missed Derek. He promised her that upon his return to Denver, he would find a way to get up to the area he thought Derek was at in Colorado. He was planning to be back in Florida in about three weeks, and he would get back up to the farm to report whatever he could on Derek's whereabouts.

Dana hated to see Gabe leave, but also couldn't wait for him to go so he could return with more news of Derek. Time stood still for Dana for the next few weeks. She was worse watching the calendar than Joy Dean was watching the widow.

Gabe started out in his little electric car for the general vicinity of where this supposed model city was located. As he traveled along in search of his friend Derek, he rethought is visit to the farm. How different the world today, and yet perhaps not so much, he mused. It was all in the way it was viewed.

Gabe recalled the surprise he felt seeing the old, blue book he had given to Mrs. Thompson laying on the table in front of the couch. He was told this was not the original, but only one of the many that was acquired and found homes through the community. It had changed their little Commune's way of thinking, as well as their personal lives. The "Course in Miracles" had become their manual for living.

So many things and lives had changed since those days. Gabe recited from memory a portion of the book that came to mind. "Appearances deceive, but can be changed. Reality is changeless. It does not deceive at all, and if you fail to see beyond appearances, you are deceived. For every thing you will see will change, and yet you thought it real before, and now you think it real again. Reality is thus reduced to form, and capable of change. Reality is changeless. It is this that makes it real, and keeps it separate from all appearances. It might transcend all form to be itself. It cannot change." Wow. I needed that jolt of reality, Gabe's inner man reminded his physical self!

He had been so lost in his thoughts he had not even noticed the miles slipping away. Then, he saw the illuminating sign stating, "Welcome to Providence, parking Terminal #2. Please be prepared to stop." Gabe saw the most beautiful, white formations reaching skyward in the background. They had crystal-like domes that were catching the sun's reflection and mirroring it back to the heavens. It was awe-inspiring!

He was approaching this huge building set right dab in the middle of the roadway. An attendant was operating some sort of electrical beam that acted like a gate. The young man welcomed Gabe to "Providence" and inquired about the nature and length of his stay. He then gave Gabe an information packet that would familiarize him with the city—both directionally and politically. It was explained that as sufficient mass transportation was provided throughout the city, private vehicles were to remain outside the city, and private vehicles were to remain outside the inner limits in well-guarded parking terminals. All public transport systems were free to city residents and visitors. Since Gabe was to be a short time visitor, he would park on the lower third level. The building had ten levels. The fourth was to accommodate incoming and outgoing freight. The freight carriers would park their cabs there and load their beds onto the rail movers to be delivered at desired delivery destinations in the city. The fifth level was the passenger area.

The attendant scanned Gabe's IDI in his hand, put a sticker on the rear bumper of the car, and motioned him on. Gabe had been informed that this building was one of four more around the city, plus the large jet port that had a monorail connection to all the gate terminals. Gabe drove cautiously to the third level and parked. He took one of the levitators to the fifth floor. There was a small lounge café, shopping area, and several refresh rooms, plus a large information booth. He stopped at the information area to inquire how to reach the home of City Director Derek Barton. He was given directions on how to proceed on the correct monorail and people trolley to the Pinnacle Building. It was explained that many of the city administrators and engineers lived there, and that since it was the tallest building in the city, he couldn't miss it.

He stepped aboard monorail #8, settled into a comfortable lounge chair, and began to observe the surroundings from the advantageous viewing position offered by the curved glass window dome of the monorail. He was really impressed so far, and the wonderment was just beginning. White granite buildings all with crystal solar paneled domes met his gaze. Scattered among the buildings were numerous landscaped parks with splashing fountains, and children playing. The monorails weaved in and around, and up and over the buildings and parks. Also noted was what appeared as early 20th century trolley cars that were taking a more leisurely approach to delivering people to selected destinations. The mono he was on made several stops, taking on and letting off passengers. It made several stops in the gigantic mall structure they had entered. People were riding moving sidewalks that had rows of plastic seats or standing areas with rails. These moving sidewalks also performed as escalators taking people to different shopping levels. There was a small park with kiddie rides, a swim and surf miniature beach, and even a small winding river with canoes and paddleboats that looked like swans on it. The best part to Gabe was the natural habitation zoo complex. And stores, with anything your heart desired, being displayed.

They were back outside the mall area now. Gabe noticed no individual land vehicles, but on quite a few of the larger buildings were what appeared to be helicopter ports. They usually had three or four of the neatest looking hover craft airships. These really caught Gabe's attention, as he was a pilot himself. He sure would like a closer look at one of those babies, he thought. Maybe, just maybe, Derek could arrange that!

The monorail came to a halt and Gabe was informed this was his stop. As he stepped out onto the marble platform, an extremely tall, impressive building caught his eye. He knew instantly that this was the Pinnacle Building. He stepped up onto the moving sidewalk and held on to the rail. The sidewalk took him right into the main lobby of the building and he stepped off. On one outer wall were eight glass-encased levitators that afforded the most fantastic view of the city. There were numerous inner levitators available also, but Gabe wanted the scenic tour.

He stepped off on floor 12, still in a daze and couldn't believe the world he had stepped off into. Was he back in ancient Greece? He wondered if he had stepped into a time capsule instead of a levitator. Marble statues, a fountain, and lush vegetation lined a marble pathway that led up to a white columned entrance. A doorman greeted Gabe. Gabe was still somewhat speechless, but managed to give his name and inquire if this was the residence of his friend.

He was ushered into this inner court that was as almost as impressive as the outer. Moments later, he heard a welcome, hearty greeting. "Gabe! Is that really you?" Gabe turned in the direction of the familiar voice. "Wow! I am dreaming!" Gabe grabbed his friend in a bear hug embrace. "Not dreaming anymore, Gabe. The dream has manifested!"

The next 24 hours catapulted Gabe into the most beautiful future he could have ever dared possible on this planet. Derek let him ride and even pilot his personal aircraft on an aerial inspection of his city.

Gabe told Derek all the changes that had taken place on the farm and with his family. Derek had tried so many times to get news of his people. He listened intently, crying a little, laughing a little, and longing to see them so much. He shared how so many times of late, Dana had been on his mind and how he had even felt she was sending him mental messages of her readiness to leave the farm.

Gabe told Taylor she was even more beautiful and that motherhood certainly agreed with her. Little Dean was a miniature Derek and he reminded Gabe of a small, Greek Adonis. Maybe it was the Grecian décor.

Gabe could hardly wait to get back to Florida to share this visit with Derek's family, and watch Dana's face as he presented the paid-in-advance air reservation for Derek's grandmother from Orlando to Providence. They had a large jet port just outside the city limits, and Derek would be waiting there with Taylor and Dean for their new family member to arrive!

18

The Reunion

CAM HAD DROPPED GABE OFF in Orlando on his way down to the Bahama section of the state. He needed to complete his unfinished business that his trip with Gabe to the farm had interrupted. He hated the long drives down and back, but always felt so vibrant and alive working this new part of Florida.

It was so beautiful here in this fertile, agricultural valley. The mountains shielded the east side of the valley from the strong Atlantic, and the gentle Gulf winds were cooled slightly as they traveled across the Okeechobee Sea. The soil that had recently been a part of the ocean floor was now the most fertile farmland in Florida.

A small but expanding city was emerging in the center of the valley. It seemed appropriate, since the Atlantic Ocean had birthed this new landmass, to name it Atlantis. Perhaps, some reasoned, an ancient namesake had a similar geographic setting.

Once again, the city fathers had not only extended an invitation, but also urged Cameron to become the District Overseer. The idea was so enticing to Cam, and even Joy Dean had warmed to the thought of relocating here. Cameron promised that he'd give them a definite decision by the end of the following week when he returned with the new shipment of hybrid seedlings.

The family, as always, was glad to see Cam return from his trips. This time, though, they felt a tenseness about him. They kept waiting for Cam to initiate, revealing the reason for his mysterious countenance. They waited until supper was finished and then sat expectantly around the table. When Cam still sat quiet, John broke the silence. "What! What is it, Cam?" "What is what, Dad?" Cam fidgeted in his seat. "What is going on in that head of yours? Out with it!" John's voice sounded very parental. "Okay." Cam cleared his throat and began, "I am seriously thinking of taking this city directors position in

Atlantis. I have a little over a week to accept or decline. I'd like to accept and want you all to consider moving there, too. They have promised us all new living quarters and living expenses, plus a vehicle." Cam paused and waited for their reactions to this announcement. He did not have a long wait, as they all began to express their feelings simultaneously.

Joy Dean and the twins were anxious to start packing. They were excited over the prospects of living in a city. John and Amy were torn between going with their family and staying in the familiar, comfortable surroundings of the farm. They final agreed they were too settled in and didn't wish to make any drastic changes in their lives, at least not yet. Dana was so fearful that Derek would return and not know where to find them. She loved her son, granddaughter, and great grandbabies dearly. But she really only had one more dream to realize before accepting her life complete. She wanted to see Derek again, and so she opted to stay with John and Amy on the farm.

Cam looked at his father-in-law sitting quietly and expressionless. "Dad Barton?" They all turned towards Devon. Joy Dean realized her dad had not spoken his thoughts yet, and she felt his strong mixture of emotions. "Dad, you know I could never move without you, nor could I enjoy our new home knowing you weren't happy there. Your feelings on this family matter are most important to Cam and me."

Devon reached over and patted his mother's hand and addressed his first comments to her. "Mom, I guess I was tuned in to your feelings more than any of the others expressed here. If you had not been there for me when we first moved to Florida, when I almost lost the farm, when I said farewell to Tamara, when the kids needed a motherly friend, when the encouragement was needed to try again, and when the farm was destroyed and rebuilt...none of us would even be here discussing our options. So I feel this is my chance to replace a small drop of "thank you" back into the barrel of love you have nourished this family with these many years. I choose to remain ere with you I also wish not to carry around needless guilt over this decision by holding Cam and Joy back from their destiny. They must go, and with our blessings." With that, Devon considered the family council meeting over and walked outside to attend to the day's chores.

Gabe landed the air freighter in Orlando, quickly processed the docking and delivery information into the computer's log, arranged for an available compact, and headed for the farm. The compacts were not noted for being speedy, but this particular vehicle seemed to be dragging an anchor of concrete. He pulled into a Service Island to get a cold beverage and check the solar cells.

He couldn't have been more surprised, for just as he opened the door to enter into the refreshment bar, he bumped into a departing customer. "Gabe?" "Cam?" They stopped and stared in disbelief. They went back inside for a quick explanation of their presence there.

Cam explained he was on his way to Atlantis to accept a new job position. He would have been more excited if only his parents and Joy's family would be receptive to moving also. Gabe said that perhaps his news would make a change, at least for Devon. He told of his visit with Derek and the flight reservation he had sent back for his grandmother. Cam agreed that this might make Devon more interested in moving. That would sure please Joy, he thought. They bid each other goodbye, Cam headed south, and Gabe continued on north to the farm.

Gabe reached the farm late afternoon. The outside humidity had limited the farm occupants to inside activities. Dana was sewing patches on the twins' blue jeans. They were really hard on clothes as their all boy games were quite stressful on clothes. They wore out clothes almost as fast as they outgrew them. Joy Dean was bathing Charity after her independent feeding attempt. John was dozing in his chair, and Amy was folding laundry. Devon was re-gluing a couple of kitchen chairs. They each were fairly conversational today and more into their own thoughts, which centered on "the move." They were all so absorbed in their own individual space that the knock on the door was not even being noticed.

Gabe pounded harder and yelled, "Anyone home?" Dana perked up her ears. "Was that Gabe's voice?" she inquired. Devon sat down the glue and walked over to open the door. Yes, there he stood once more in the doorway, grinning. All were excited to see him, but none as much as Dana. Before Devon could offer him a chair or Amy approach him with a cold drink, Dana began to pump him for information about Derek.

Gabe really drew out the story and covered every detail of his visit, of the city, of Derek's living quarters, of Taylor and little Dean, but withheld the big surprise for the grand finale!

"Are they going to be able to visit us soon?" Dana questioned. She had enjoyed Gabe's accounting of his visit, but it had only served to increase her longing to see Derek. "Well, he is very busy and has a lot of responsibilities in his city, so I doubt if he can get away," Gabe teased. He could feel Dana's disappointment and knew it was time to let her in on the surprise. "Since Derek won't be able to come here..." Gabe paused just a moment for the big crescendo, "he wants you to come to them!" Gabe pulled out the reservation and handed it to Dana.

Dana's moment had arrived, her dream realized, and all she could do was look at the plastic card that would unite her and her grandson and cry tears of joy.

Derek had sent word by Gabe for his grandmother to only pack a few cherished belongings for her city wardrobe. Except for some family photographs, a box of Dean's letters from Vietnam, some personal souvenirs, jewelry pieces, her Bible, the "Course in Miracles" book, and a few toiletry articles, she was ready. Gabe had told her she would fly out the date on her reservation, which was only a couple days away, and that her new family would meet her in Providence.

She was sorry to miss saying goodbye to Cameron, but she did ask Devon to reconsider going with Joy now. She said she knew how much it meant to Joy. Joy had always prided herself as her father's caretaker, and she had been. But Devon had always been the influence behind Joy's achievements, her confident supporter. They needed each other. Devon said he would give it serious thought.

Devon and Joy Dean planned to take Dana to the air terminal in Orlando. Then, they were planning to drive over to Atlantis to allow Devon to see the area first hand. Besides, Joy missed Cam.

It was late in the afternoon and even though it was still warm, Dana wanted to walk one more time down to the pond. Devon walked her down to their bench. They sat there very quietly for a while, and then Dana spoke. "Wherever you are, my son, wherever you go, you are protected and safe in the love of the Eternal. I am so honored to have been allowed to share this Earth-walk with you, your children, and their children. I have been blessed with an abundance of friends and good neighbors. I give thanks for each one. Love knows no barriers, no distances, and no limitations. My love I leave with you; your love I take with me. I'm ready now to say my farewells to this farm. I bless it and all who know and will share their energies with it." They walked back to the house in silence. All that needed to be said had been.

Hugs and goodbyes to her dearest friends, John and Amy. Well wishes to all the members of the little Commune. Tears and kisses to each of the twins and Charity. She locked their sweet faces in her innermost chamber of memories. She then climbed into the front seat beside Devon. Joy was waving to her children who would stay with Amy. It was something Joy had never done before, to leave the children for a few days. She was torn between seeing Grandma Dana off and seeing Cam, or jumping out to remain with her babies. The car moved down the drive, but no heads turned to look back. They just didn't trust their emotions. The journey had begun.

Dana gazed around her comfortable surroundings. She was seated in a most comfortable reclining lounge chair. If she tilted it back, she could gaze right out into the heavens through the sturdy, plexi-dome observatory section of the aircraft. This was truly prime seating Derek had arranged for her. The aircraft had two and a half levels. The observatory sat almost over the pilots' chamber.

Dana had been assisted to the upper level and to seat 215, her reserved seat, by the most pleasant and courteous male attendant. He showed her how to adjust her seat and attached the safety take off and landing straps. He assisted in the hook up and said after they reached cruising altitude, he would be back to release it.

Dana felt the aircraft lift off, and she watched the landscape of Florida miniaturize. It was getting dusk and soon the stars were easier to see than the disappearing land. Dana knew she was really saying goodbye to Florida. It had been the stage her life had played on for the most of her Earth time. The really important parts of her life were traveling with her. She would cherish and carry these memories right over to the "other side." She could never leave them behind, for they were more than memories—they had become Dana.

She didn't have too long to visit the past in her mind; it was too actively absorbed in participating in the now. She felt like a schoolgirl waiting for her prom date. She wondered if Derek had changed much—if he was still as sensitive—and if they would be able to resume their closeness, or if time would have created a void that would need to be refilled. She wondered if Taylor would really be as congenial with a live-in grandmother as with a visiting one. Who would Dean look like, and would he take right up with her? Oh, you really are a silly goose! she thought. Here you are, right on the doorstep of your dream, and you are projecting a suitcase full of mental monsters. Besides, how could any person contemplate anything but goodness while viewing the mystical beauty of the night sky? The stars reminded Dana how eternal life was, how endless the universe, and how much a part of it all she was.

She was so tuned in to the lights of the heavens above that she was not aware the craft had begun its decent. She heard the pilot's voice alerting them to their soon arrival at Providence, and hoped their fight had been pleasant.

The craft was nosing downward and the view of the heavens suddenly became upstaged! Dana witnessed the most dazzling, breathtaking sight of her life! This had to be the sight Derek had witnessed in his dream, she thought. She wondered if perhaps she was dreaming. This was too awesome to be real.

The attendant was bending over and helping to fasten the safety belt for landing. He caught Dana's look of enchantment and said, "I always get the same spellbinding feeling no matter how many times I view it." "Yes, Dana agreed. "I think I've just been raptured and this must be Heaven!" "Perhaps it is a little bit of Heaven, and if the world proves itself worth this time," the attendant stated, "Heaven will visit Earth more often. We can hope, can't we?" The attendant patted Dana's hand, grinned, and disappeared down the stairwell.

Afterword

THE STORY WAS COMPLETE and the author satisfied it was good enough to share with her world with the exception of a title. It became a frustrating endeavor, as it would be the enticing door to lead potential readers to venture into the awaiting story pages—or not. Though some fairly good runners up, nothing seemed right until a Higher Energy moment directed attention to the first and last chapters of the story. They described a futuristic city of hope so needed by a world that had been plagued by many emotional tests and hardships.

The name of this city of hope is Providence. I wondered if the name had a meaning. I looked up the word "Providence" in the Webster Dictionary and I quote the finding: "timely preparatory for future eventualities." I felt a Divine confirmation that I knew the title to this book...*Providence.*

About The Author

June E. Summers

I'VE SEEN AND SHARED over 80 years of making memory time capsules. Earlier years created a sense of feeling loved and safe. But by my mid-life years, it was more like a rollercoaster ride—somewhere between exhilarating and frightening.

My 40 and 50 years of living were more internalized into discovering who and why I was.

My 60 through 70-year span was a mixture of saying goodbye to family members and a few friends. Also, quite a few hellos and welcome to newly arriving ones.

My 80s have been a period of letting go of past living standards, such as home ownership, driving my car, and healthy mind and body. My children became more parental and I more dependent on them.

I am grateful they each made this transitional time with the purest motive of Love—and that is like my story *Providence.* It ends with hope materializing, and Love. That is how I expect my life's closure to be. May the Creator of this planet's population awaken us to "love thy neighbor as thyself" and care for this Earth we have neglected for so long. Let your personal Creator always be your Engineer. Even over the bumps.